Walk the Darkness Down

Walk the Darkness Down

A Novel

Daniel Magariel

BLOOMSBURY PUBLISHING
NEW YORK · LONDON · OXFORD · NEW DELHI · SYDNEY

BLOOMSBURY PUBLISHING
Bloomsbury Publishing Inc.
1385 Broadway, New York, NY 10018, USA

BLOOMSBURY, BLOOMSBURY PUBLISHING, and the Diana logo are
trademarks of Bloomsbury Publishing Plc

First published in the United States 2023

LIBRARY OF CONGRESS CATALOGING-IN-PUBLICATION DATA IS AVAILABLE

ISBN: HB: 978-1-63557-814-0; EBOOK: 978-1-63557-815-7

2 4 6 8 10 9 7 5 3 1

Typeset by Westchester Publishing Services
Printed and bound in the U.S.A.

To find out more about our authors and books visit www.bloomsbury.com and
sign up for our newsletters.

Bloomsbury books may be purchased for business or promotional use. For
information on bulk purchases please contact Macmillan Corporate and Premium
Sales Department at specialmarkets@macmillan.com.

For Justine

All unavoided is the doom of destiny.

——SHAKESPEARE, *RICHARD III*

ONE

He's just through the front door of the apartment and Marlene's spitting and slapping, asking, Where the hell you been? Les sweeps past her and she follows him into the hallway, the living room, the kitchen, refusing to let up. He flings open the cabinet beneath the sink, pulls out a black fifty-gallon trash bag. She's on top of him, pressing, Where do you think you're going now? He slips by her again, the kind of caustic boredom in his face that he knows makes her want to take a swing at the back of his head. He moves to the dryer where he starts stuffing his clean clothes into the trash bag for the boat's early-morning departure. She follows him still.

What's changed? he asks. Nothing.

I only wanted to talk tonight.

We've been having this same conversation for years.

It'd be a way forward for us.

Why would we ever go back?

Why would we stay in this Neverland?

I'm not moving down there. The crew needs me. I have a responsibility to them.

And what about to me?

They're family.

Family?

Family.

I see, she says, calming, a curve of sadness in her eyes. I asked you to bring me home flowers tonight. I said I'd make dinner. I thought we could take a bath.

Sex has become primitive to him, violent, grisly as a knifing.

Plus there's the hostility implied in her suggestion. She's daring him to touch her, with tenderness, knowing full well how difficult it would be for them both.

Please, she says, her hand held out. I really just wanted to talk tonight.

She walks him to the dining room table and pulls out a chair.

He sets his trash bag by his side, knowing that by morning, once his mind is clear, he will look upon these hours different. He will regret staying out and storming in and sleeping on the trawler tonight, awakening tomorrow stiff and drawn at the first pink of dawn—that's when he will see his wife through the wound and rot of loss. But right now, with white-rimmed nostrils and a handle half gone, he is free to hate her with the force of his soul.

He stares straight ahead, eyes glittering and indignant.

Tiny flames hang above the burned-down candlesticks, pewter-rimmed plates ringed in fire, the warm aromas of slow-cooked flesh. Music floats pendulously through the apartment and the tired night sighs with a dry wheeze.

MARLENE SITS BESIDE him, taking a moment to collect her thoughts, to reorganize the lines she's rehearsed. She wants to disarm him, to shake him at his core, to tell him something raw and not quite formed. To reach inside herself and grasp some truth just on the verge of discovery. You remember the first month with her, the three of us together? she asks. In the old home. There was no past there. No future. It was pure. Those were the only happy moments I ever had in this town. There's nothing here anymore. Nothing for me, anyway. For anyone except all you lost boys refusing to grow up. Take a moment and think about that. Don't answer with your animal brain. What does the man inside you say? I gave up my dream for you. What'd you ever give up?

Flames swim in his watery eyes and she believes that she's captured his attention, that he recalls all that purpose burning bright as diamonds on the walls of their dim cave.

We need to go back, she says. I can't explain it. But it's time to go back.

She touches his cheek, then puts her hand on his heart.

She spreads her palm to capture its full warmth and rhythm.

He's sweating, she notices.

His gaze distant, dilated.

Did you do drugs tonight? she asks.

Marlene presses her hand firmly to his chest.

His face hardens, heart continuing to race.

She asks him to respond.

He does not respond.

Are you kidding me? she says, her voice rising. Are you fucking kidding me?

And he's up out of his chair, past her again, trash bag in hand.

She follows him to their bedroom, where he forces the door closed, locking her out.

She hurls a shoulder into the door.

You're a child. You're all a bunch of children.

She continues to fling herself into the door, each time with less restraint.

The hinges tear and she falls through, landing at his feet.

She reaches for his legs as he steps over her.

She digs a fingernail into his trash bag, rips it open.

Les grabs all he can from what she's torn from the bag and then he's out the front door, starting back down the exterior stairwell when she throws herself on him and they tumble to the bottom. Her head almost smacks the railing. Her forearms rake the cement.

He squirms out from beneath her.

She rages, flails her limbs, twists her trunk as he holds her to the ground.

He begs her to calm down, pleads with her.

Dammit, he says, you're going to wake up—

He stops himself.

She quits fighting, lets her back go slack, allowing his hand to press her face into the freezing asphalt. For a moment she believes he might somehow conjure Angie by uttering her name, which he's refused to do for two years now. For a moment, turning her eyes to the top of the stairs, to all the light pouring out of their apartment, she stakes her life on the doorway not being empty.

TWO

The next night, Marlene fans a blanket out over a woman's lap, warming her bare legs, making her comfortable. Les is at sea, the apartment now Marlene's alone. She drops to a knee, unstraps the woman's clear spike-heeled pumps and slips them off, places each foot on the towel she's laid over the cold swept floor. She stands, steps to the stove where the kettle whistles softly. She pours hot water into a basin, wets a wash rag, swishing it with soap until the cloth is loaded with suds. She carries these things back to the kitchen table and, dropping to her knees a second time, arranges them on the floor. She then washes the feet of her guest as if those of a saint.

Finished, Marlene lets them soak. In the bathroom she pulls Vaseline from the medicine cabinet. She returns to the kitchen, rips a paper towel from the roll, folds and licks the seam, tears the sheet into quarters. She dabs the paper towel in the Vaseline and leans in close to the woman, attempting to wipe away the suffocating cake of makeup.

The woman recoils, starts to say something.

Hush, Marlene says. Hush.

Marlene tries again.

The woman shudders a second time.

Please, Marlene says. You'll sleep here tonight. I'll pay.

The woman settles into her chair, and Marlene proceeds to lay bare the details of her face. The worry lines of her forehead Marlene excavates with a pass over the brow. High subtle cheekbones and thin taut lips beneath the dramatic blush and penciled outline of her lipstick. The woman's eyes dulling to gray-blue once clean of eye shadow and mascara. But it's the tiny cuts on her cheeks, pinprick acne scars and other slight quarter-inch etchings, that most appeal to Marlene. They give her guest a pimply adolescence, a long-nailed sibling—a time before this time. On nights like these Marlene sees herself as a kind of archaeologist, exhuming the lives of others. As Marlene works, the woman she picked up an hour ago is remade into a girl, not much more than twenty, a soft smile on her naked mouth, on her right cheek the faintest dimple.

Marlene smiles back.

She spent the night as she often did with Les gone. She drove around town, lingering until near day in empty streetlight-lit parking lots, staring hypnotically into windows and storefronts, where memories of her daughter once flickered. A fourth birthday at Drama Kids in preparation for which Angie insisted on making her costume from scratch. And the playground injury to her chin, her only stitches, when she braved a walk up the slide as another kid came down. But Angie had long since refused to come out of the shadows, despite Marlene's wish to once again be her audience.

Dark crept in off the sea, the cold seizing town.

Beneath streetlamps, snow whirled like schools of fish.

Marlene, not ready to return home, drove the forty-five minutes to The Villas.

A two-story L-shaped doo-wop relic complete with a towering neon sign of palm trees, sand, and sea, the motel, once bustling with seasonal renters, now charges for rooms by the hour. Warm weather, the women stand out on the street or sunbathe around the pool that lay dry year-round. Winter, they keep to the lobby, taking shifts in the bus stop enclosure just across from the motel, four or five at a time huddling together on display, like reproductions in a bizarre museum diorama. She parked a block away, headlights off, window cracked, smoking Merits. There were no cars in the parking lot tonight, just three women in the bus stop, all of whom she recognized. Marlene took care to go unnoticed: She never entered the motel, never even pulled up to the lobby, and never brought home the same woman twice. She lit another cigarette with the butt of the last, settled into her seat to wait for the shift change, for a new girl to exit the motel and sub out another in the bus stop, before she slipped the car into drive, flicked on her headlights, and rolled cautiously up to the enclosure.

She leads the girl to the bathroom, turns the water to a comfortable temperature, hands her a towel, robe, hanger, invites her to take a bath. In the kitchen she moves the soup she made earlier in the day to a front burner. She turns on the gas, strikes a match to light the stove, then a smoke with the same flame. She preps everything she needs for dinner before sitting down to the table with a bag of apples and a paring knife. She turns over the newspaper to the article she's been flipping to for several nights:

Five Thousand Red-winged Blackbirds Fall from the Sky

The image is of a field in a neighboring county dotted with broken, contorted carcasses: some on their backs, taking in the upside-down world; some doubled over about to sit up or straighten out; yet others embraced in the fold of another's wing, huddling as if for warmth. Among the dead is one that captures Marlene's eye. On its stomach, wings and tail spread full, red and yellow shoulder bars magnificent as war paint, the bird appears to glide just above a snow-dusted stretch. The article quotes someone calling the event *biblical*.

The bathroom door opens.

Marlene jumps and flips back over the paper, steps to the stove to stir the soup.

There's quiet behind her, silence, no floor creak.

She turns.

The girl stands in the doorframe of the bathroom, wet hair combed back and dripping, a sensual slant to her body. Robe draped wide at the shoulders, tied lazily at the waist.

A mistake made by some of the women Marlene brought home.

Marlene starts to say something.

Hush, the girl says. Hush.

She lets the robe fall.

The childishness of her front—flat chest and absent hair— lights a sudden fury in Marlene.

Fuck sake, she snaps. Cover up that plucked chicken and come get a bite to eat.

SHE EATS EVERYTHING in silence, the only sounds in the apartment the scrape of the utensil against her teeth and the on-off rhythm of the central heat and the sleet spattering the skylight. There is soup to start, rich and delicious, fried pork chops with caramelized onions, scallops sautéed in butter, stewed tomatoes, and, for dessert, tea, apple pie, cherries.

Marlene stands in the corner. They do not say a word.

She's made a habit of not engaging with these women—no names, no personal details, no unnecessary chatter. She prefers the mystery of their quiet company. But Marlene did not mean to offend her and the girl did not take the insult lightly. She reeled, covering her body with her hands, dropped down to the floor to reclaim the robe, and stepped guardedly to her place setting at the table. Marlene watches her eat now, a steady ribbon of smoke unraveling from a cigarette. The girl is skinny but the heartiness of her appetite charms Marlene. The girl's eyes continue to peer at the bedroom entrance, just off the kitchen, the door caved in.

Marlene clears away the dishes.

The room becomes tidy.

She lights another Merit.

How was the food? Marlene asks.

The girl smiles politely.

You can say something.

The girl holds her silence.

Say something, please. I didn't mean to hurt your feelings.

The girl looks to the bedroom, nods to the busted door. When's he coming back?

That was me.

Doesn't seem like you.

Excuse me?

We talk about you, you know? The girl points to her heels by the table. We wear clear.

What else do *we* say?

That you're a good cook. And you don't talk much. Bill knows about you too. He looks closer than most people, sees what others can't. One night his soul left his body right in front of me. True story. Swear. I mean, I didn't actually see it leave. I was there, though, and we were done using drugs back then and everything. We were just sitting in the car and he looked up and his soul was

9

trying to climb out the window. He scolded it like a child, saying, *Get back down here in this body.* And it did. It listened. Ever since, he can see things, like colors around people, their orals.

Silence resets the room.

You didn't smile, the girl says. You were supposed to smile. I know it's *auras.* But I'll say that for the longest time I thought my grandma died of Old Timer's disease. And that the veins on her legs were Very Close Veins. There's another one, too, almost broke my heart. I've heard all my life that it's a Doggy Dog World, which seemed kind of sweet. Like a slobbery, goofy world where a bunch of puppies with big tongues and big paws stumble around. But Bill explained the saying was Dog Eat Dog, which isn't nearly as nice.

Marlene nods, attentive to the up inflection the girl makes at the end of each sentence, as if every assertion is a question and Marlene has to make clear she's following.

A moment later the girl asks, Do you have any ice cream?

Marlene can't help but laugh.

She pulls a carton from the freezer, a spoon from the drawer, hands them to the girl.

Marlene takes a seat next to her at the table.

After the first bite, the girl sighs with pleasure and scoops out another.

I used to growl whenever my grandmother fed me ice cream as a baby, the girl says. It's how I let her know that I wanted more. I mean, besides the fact that you shouldn't feed ice cream to a baby, just forget about that one detail a minute, but that I knew I liked it so much that I'd found a way to tell her even as an infant. It's kind of like this cat I used to have, whenever the water in the bowl was gone, he'd just swipe at the bowl over and over, making this kind of pretty paw-against-glass sound like a wind chime, almost. I mean, well, actually, it wasn't pretty at all. It was annoying as hell, especially in the middle of the night. But still the cat had trained me to know that that sound meant to get your butt out of bed and get me some water. Like me growling: Just dig that spoon into that carton one more time, Grandma, and feed me some more of that sugary deliciousness. She's gone now. Did I say that?

The girl shifts in her seat, apologizes for talking too much.

She communes with some private thought.

Show me, Marlene says.

No, come on.

Marlene grasps the girl's hand, slips the spoon from her grip, scoots closer.

Go on, now, show me.

She raises the spoon to the girl's mouth.

The girl takes a bite, tries to growl. No, that's not right.

Marlene feeds her a second bite.

A grunt this time, low and from the diaphragm.

That's not it either.

A soft almost-purr follows the third.

There, she says. Closer, anyway.

Again, Marlene says. Show me again.

Marlene offers another spoonful.

The girl growls a fourth time.

That's it, she says. That's the one.

Marlene screeches with joy: Again, again, again.

The girl takes another bite.

Again, again, again.

The girl laughs, too, swept up with enthusiasm.

Growl, growl, Marlene says, slapping the table, encouraging her more and more feverishly, the girl quickening the pace, bites coming faster now, the growls transforming into a continuous, guttural hum. They are both lost in the moment, unable to stop until the carton is empty, exuberance fading to exhaustion, and the echo of Marlene's voice hangs over them like a sickly song, Growl, growl, she cries. Growl, Angie, growl.

THE REST OF the night they watch TV on the couch. The girl, resting her head on Marlene's lap, nods off just before daybreak. Marlene sinks into her seat, fingers combing through her hair, thoughts lost in the comfort of someone sleeping close. Les wouldn't approve. In her mind his voice sounds a lot like her mother's. You ought seek counseling again; this is grief gone awry. But who is she harming? He's out scalloping, which is where he always convinced himself he needed to be, so she will do as she pleases. She turns her head to the ceiling, across which the red-winged blackbirds come upon the town like a storm. One by one at first, slapping a roof, a sidewalk, a windshield, and then falling in numbers, assaulting the earth. She remains like that until morning seeps in from the edges of the blinds and the streetlamps just outside the apartment click off and the engines of the work-bound cars a floor below start up and Marlene shuts her eyes, too, drifting into tomorrow.

THREE

The day dawns calm. Les watches sunup from his box at the stern, the only outdoor cutting station onboard, where he posts rain and shine, day and night. The rest of the crew he calls *Housecats* for their need of shelter in the shucking room. They've called him *Stray* since he was young. A cigarette dangling from his lips, he presses each shell to his abdomen, slips his knife in from the side, scrapes the blade across the roof, popping open the scallop. His next motion he scoops out the guts, knifes the meat into a bucket, flings the shell and innards back to the sea. The birds caw and wheel and dive after the scraps, a pitchy swarm trailing the boat by the hundreds.

This trip he refuses to wear a belly guard while shucking. He wants the distraction of pain, the hateful swirl of color. Over the course of a week, by simply pressing one shell after another into his stomach, which is the only way to leverage the scallops open, the bruise has continued to creep, the purples and reds and yellows to darken, to deepen. It's a way to keep thoughts of Marlene at bay. But the same repetitive cutting motion that breaks down the body also breaks down the mind: Out on the stern he lives inside himself for hours at a time, replaying the ugliness of their fight, resurfacing from the downward spiral of his reflections only when his shame manifests into a wince or shake of the head or grit of the teeth. He awakens then to the frigid day before him, grateful for the reprieve, for the cold, the birds, and he thrusts another shell into his stomach, steers his focus back to the warm throb of his wound.

The crew hazing New Guy this trip granted some distraction too.

Still, Les wishes John Wayne hadn't slapped the kid.

Yesterday afternoon when the draggers came up, the starboard dredge was flipped. The crew welcomed the rest. Captain Alright reset the dredge. China shuffled a deck of waterproof playing cards. John Wayne reclined in sunshine, wolfing down a box of kid's cereal out of a large mixing bowl. Hoover boasted of his keenness to vacuum another paycheck up his nose. Booby, Hoover's uncle and the boat's first mate, hit his hands once more with the last of his pain ointment and tossed the tube overboard. Les hung upside down, gravity boots fastened to a beam off the flounder nets, a Merit in his teeth. The blood rush and muscle stretch another welcome relief. Meanwhile, they forced New Guy to sort the half load alone—shells into a bucket, bi-catch shoveled off deck—as they jeered at him from the sidelines.

How many times I tell you to stop picking just the tops of piles, Hoover said.

You got to sort all the way to the bottom, Booby shouted. Get lower.

China shoved in next to the kid, fanned his playing cards out on deck, started snatching them up fast one at a time, mocking New Guy for how slow he was at picking. While bent over, he saw a large scallop the kid overlooked. Hey, Stevie Wonder, can you afford to leave money on deck? I sure as fuck can't.

They'd been out ten watches so far, just about eight days, the seven-man crew long since exchanging the sun and stars for a fourteen and six work-rest cycle. In all that time New Guy still hadn't observed that the proper form was to bend at the hips, not the knees. He'd been doing a half-squat position for days, grabbing the rail to hold up his exhausted legs. Apart from China—who despite the nickname was Vietnamese and from San Jose—the rest of the crew cut their teeth on this very boat, Les's father and Booby their elder tormentors. They'd been hazed the same way New Guy was being hazed. The philosophy was simple: Learn the right way of doing things by studying those around you. Until then, New Guy could blame himself for his own suffering.

Mister, you'd better find another line of work. This one sure don't fit your pistol, John Wayne said, adding the film attribution: The Shootist, 1976.

Kid's going to collapse into the pile, said Booby. If he doesn't start paying attention.

You see the teeth on that monkfish? Hoover pointed. That's the one going to take your face. Or maybe an ear. Not like they're any use to you.

Cheek Meat, Les chimed in, there's a good one for the kid.

Hoover slapped his knee. You all hear what Stray called him? Cheek Meat. Called him

Cheek Meat. Dang, that's good.

They all laughed, chanting, Cheek Meat.

The new nickname inspired the next round of torment: monkfish competition.

Les declared himself the judge, preferring to remain hanging.

Hundred a person, China suggested.

They all agreed on twenty bucks.

Booby volunteered to go first.

The game kicked off as the old man burst a monkfish's eyeballs with two quick stabs of his knife. He then stuck his thumb and first finger into the sockets, lifted and steadied the flailing fish on the rail. He slit from fin to gill on one side and the other. A third cut down the underbelly spilled the pink-orange guts out on deck. His arthritic hands quivering from the strain, he took extra time sawing the vertebra, the fish fighting him until its spine finally snapped.

Hoover used a similar method but skipped the stabbing step. He jammed his fingers into the eye sockets instead, then elected to break the vertebra with a swift sudden fist. His motions convulsive, efficient, surprisingly loud.

John Wayne retied the bandana around his forehead and tucked his beard into his weatherproof overalls before handling his monkfish. His knife work was as precise as Hoover's except a live crab fell from his fish's intestines and, trailing bile, scurried away. John Wayne stomped the crab, insisted on bonus points for killing two things rather than one.

Half the weight of John Wayne, China didn't bother lifting the fish at all. He kicked his boot into the monkfish's mouth instead and, grabbing its tail, cut across the midsection. He raised the prize triumphantly, flicked the severed head off his boot, sent it whirling across deck, mouth open and teeth barred, bowels uncoiling. The fish head teetered on the edge of the scupper before dropping back to the sea.

That's the West Coast special, motherfuckers, China said.

That's some Far East TONC shit, Booby said.

Cut out that racist TONC shit, China said.

There ain't enough meat on that tail, Hoover insisted.

Bullshit, China said. Pay up.

Let Stray decide, John Wayne said.

Les examined the tail, turning it over, blood drying fast on his hands, sticking to the filter of his cigarette. He took his time and drew out the drama.

Disqualified, he proclaimed.

Uproar across deck, laughter.

Cheek Meat tried last. His first few stabs, he missed the eyes, stuck the skull instead. The monk fish, mouth open, raring to tear, kicked its tail, following him as he sidestepped for better angles. The crew cheered him on. Encouraged, Cheek Meat improvised, driving the knife through the monk fish's mouth, pinning its jaw to the deck. With a second knife he pulled from his coveralls, he blinded the fish. Next, he spilled out the guts in three slits, as the others had done. While he worked, the kid swept his tongue across the grin of his lips.

Hoover said, Maybe the kid's got the stuff.

John Wayne said, He ain't as short on ears as we thought.

Even Booby and China agreed.

Les was the only one alarmed by the desperation with which the kid craved attention.

As Cheek Meat sawed into the vertebra his hand grew tired on the rail, started shaking, the fish fighting him now. His knife wasn't working cleanly through the bone, and the crew turned on him quick. The kid's face went dour, half grin gone. Left was the uneven grit of his teeth and beads of sweat on his lip.

Fuck's the point of owning a knife too dull to cut? Hoover said.

Cheek Meat lost himself to anger, started sticking the monk-fish all over.

He let the fish drop to deck, heel-stomped the spine until it snapped.

The crew silent again.

No one knew what to say.

Les, hanging there, fell further into reflection by the explosion of violence. The upside-down world somehow stayed put for a moment and he marveled how the entire crew were not just now plunging from these great heights down into the bright marsh of clouds below.

Monk Man! Hoover shouted, breaking the silence.

Monk Man, they all agreed.

The boat lurched. The engine downshifted.

The crank of the boom and the shriek of the lines began.

Les swung himself up, unhitched his boots from the beam.

Captain Alright came over the intercom. Alright, let's get back to work, alright?

Alright, Captain Alright, they said together.

None of the small stuff, alright?

Alright, Captain Alright.

You bastards never had a lesson in this life.

Alright, Captain Alright.

The tops of the drags broke the water's surface and swung onboard, Alright orchestrating it all from the haul-back station, hands on joysticks. Hoover and China clipped up the dredges. Seafloor life squirmed in the sparkling chainmesh nets and Alright spilled out the catch, two slick wriggling piles on either side of the deck.

John Wayne, China, and Booby sorted the portside haul.

Les, Hoover, and Monk Man took starboard.

From the top of the pile the kid pulled up a behemoth, forty-or-so-pound lobster.

He held it high, called out to the crew.

Hey, hey, lookee, lookee.

Lobster rolls, Hoover said excited.

Fuck that mayonnaise shit, Booby said.

Lobster that size, meats too tough for anything else.

Just no greens, John Wayne said. I don't eat the food that my food eats.

You just ate a entire box of cereal, Booby said. There's grains and shit in that.

My food doesn't eat cereal, does it, old man?

How 'bout tacos! China said, asking for grief.

What is wrong with you? Booby asked. There's some Prego. We'll make Italian.

It's fucking lobster, Chef Boyardee, Hoover said.

You really are strange as blue-footed booby, China said.

It wasn't the bird I was nicknamed after.

Come on. That true? China asked the crew. How'd Booby get his nickname?

They used to call him Cyclops on account the glass eye, Hoover said.

You got a glass eye? Monk asked.

My old man gave him the name Booby, Les said. Over some broad.

She wasn't just *some* broad, Stray, Booby said. Her name was Sheila. She'd had a single mastectomy. And what a booby it was. I left my third wife for her. The crew broke out in laughter. She's gone now. Cancer came back.

They went quiet again.

Les nudged Monk, pointed to the lobster.

Turn her over, he said.

Along the lobster's underside hundreds of black eggs hung in vine clusters.

Jesus, Monk said. Look at 'em all.

Amazing, right?

Yeah, man, amazing.

Go on, toss her back.

Monk lifted the lobster up higher.

Caviar, he shouted, pretending to tongue the eggs.

What did I just say to you?

It's lobster. I'm not throwing it back.

Toss her back.

Monk held the eggs closer to his open mouth. What would you all give me? Twenty? Fifty?

Not everything is a joke! Les suddenly yelled. Not everything's fun and games. You aren't paying attention. You aren't taking this shit serious. Acting stupid's how people get hurt.

The kid was confused after Les's eruption, eyes darting around deck for allies.

He looked to the rail where they had just gambled over savaging the monk fish.

Go easy, kid, John Wayne said. Stray's right. What he's saying is important.

Toss her back, Les said, still burning hot.

Monk turned to the crew.

What the fuck is Stray's problem? he asked.

John Wayne slapped him.

A wild, untamed fury swam in the water pooling in the kid's eyes, like he was staring down a man who'd hit him before. What the hell was that for? I didn't even say nothing to you, Monk screamed. He took a step back to the rail, bent over to set the lobster down, and swung up swiftly, hurling the lobster high into the sky before it splashed back into the sea.

Les dragged John Wayne to the bow before he could reach the kid.

He loaded a bowl they kept hidden from Alright.

The kid's not right, John Wayne said.

Like you never poured salt on a slug.

That's the kind of boy that put cats in the oven.

Les laughed.

He just needs to be shown.

Not everybody's worth saving, Stray.

They stood there passing the pipe back and forth.

How's Kathleen? Les asked.

Fuck you, man. How's Marlene?

Hey.

What?

Peace on the boat when there's hell at home.

I only hit the kid because I thought you were about to.

They were too stoned to keep talking, attention too bright to head back down to the deck.

They leaned into the rail, looked out over the water together.

For years Les felt farthest from home whenever the boat trawled west. On these occasions he posted at his cutting station, staring east off the stern, looking out onto the sprawling reaches of an Atlantic unknown to him. Whenever the boat dragged east, away from land, his cutting station then facing west, he imagined he could see his girls in the offing, seated at the kitchen table or playing in the yard, waving him to return. It was a trick of perception that no longer helped him through hard days scalloping. He was at sea when he learned of his daughter's accident, the girls down in Destiny, visiting Marlene's parents. Captain Alright received the call on the satellite phone. Les stumbled out to the bow, hands clenched to the rail, fire blanket donned for warmth, for forty-three hours straight, facing west as the boat steamed west. The entire ride home the elements conspired against him. The cold wild wind remained on his face. The surface waves turned against the boat, frayed across the hull. The sun outpaced them to the horizon and almost lapped the boat a second time. The dark taunted him too. Stars tore loose and swept west across the night. Still, he remained, facing down the gathering distance, spirit unbroken, certain his child could never die.

His arms lift as if to shrug the fire blanket from his shoulders.

Les is back on the stern, daybreak before him.

He grimaces at the memory of that boat ride. He shakes his head at the recent fight with Marlene. He clenches his knife at the image of the pregnant lobster cracking the hard surface of the water. He only wanted to teach the kid, show him some limits. There's stillness in the blush of morning, and Les is grateful for the reprieve, for the cold, the birds, and he thrusts another shell into his stomach, steers his focus back to the warm throb of his wound. The day dawns calm.

FOUR

The EMERGENCY sign stands out against the night. Light from inside the hospital spills onto the street. Beneath the awning gusts of wind lift yesterday's snow off the blacktop like steam. Indoors, names rumble flatly from the intercom, coins slot into the vending machine, the smell of antiseptic and coffee. A homeless man peels off a bloody sock, hums a jaunty tune free of sorrow. An orderly guides a squeaky-wheeled gurney, the patient looking up to the stained ceiling tiles. A middle-aged couple holds hands, tired eyes peeled on a corner TV set. The security guard leans into the nurses' station, flirting. Marlene keeps tab on the theater from a seat in the corner, a magazine open on her lap, a surgical mask to obscure her face.

Earlier she visited the department store where Angie once got lost, the windows and doors now boarded. The entire strip mall shuttered aside from a post office and a dollar store repurposed into a Christian center. Marlene sat there for hours, rows of streetlamps lighting the parking lot like an abandoned runway. Angie had slipped away from Marlene and Nana inside the store, the two shouting for her until everyone took on their terror and helped search, the manager locking the doors and paging her name. Then someone heard giggling beneath a dressing rack and she came out waving like a little celebrity. Tonight, like previous nights, her daughter declined to exit the store, to strut down the sidewalk and shine up at her grandmother, asking, astonished, how so many people inside knew her name.

Next, Marlene tried the hospital where Angie had been born.

Breech through the last week, her daughter took the full term and never turned. At first Marlene was devastated to not experience a natural birth, but in the end the cesarean was an uncomplicated conclusion to what was a relatively uncomplicated pregnancy. The cramps and the constipation, the sleepiness and the restlessness, the noxious gas, the quitting cigs cold, the refusing of even a single Tylenol, the doctors trying to flip Angie like a stuck screw—she endured it all without much trouble, assured by the fact that she ate well and that she read a few informative books her mother bought for her, capping most days with the soothing ritual of a nightly bath. She claimed only a small measure of credit, then, when Angie appeared already weeks-old at birth, eyes wide-awake and a mouth wide with joy.

The complications were all with Les.

They'd met the year before in Destiny. Marlene worked part-time handling the books for her family's lumber company, part-time waitressing at a hotel pool bar during peak season, when suddenly ordering *dealer's choice* was a teeth-grinning barrel of a man introducing himself and his quiet friend as John Wayne and Stray.

Fishermen on vacation? she asked.

The lords of the village, John Wayne said, taking a bow. How'd you know?

She looked down at Les's hands, his thumb split deep and dry.

It's a beautiful day, she said, and there's a beach right across the street.

What are you driving at? John Wayne asked.

Fishermen hate the beach for some reason, she said.

John Wayne slapped the bar top, laughing. That's true. Isn't that true?

Stray nodded and smiled.

It's a nice smile, she said, the remark surprising her.

He went shy, covering his mouth.

John Wayne shook his head.

Will you stop flirting with our new friend, Stray?

I think I'm the one flirting with him, she said.

John Wayne and Stray never made it to the beach that trip as far as she could tell. They spent their days at the bar, took their meals there too. When Marlene showed up for work, Stray would

already be lounging poolside or sitting at a stool in board shorts, drinking coffee and pretending to meditate on the sea. This last pretense she found endearing. Throughout the day most of the conversations Marlene had were with John Wayne, who became a sort of greeter to all who stepped to the bar. Stray struggled to maintain the smallest bit of small talk aside from ordering a drink or requesting a napkin. All but for a few instances.

You live down here? he asked her the second day.

I grew up here.

Do you like it?

I love it.

Why do you love it?

You don't think it's nice?

Sure I do.

Then why are you asking?

I was just wondering about you, he said. What it's like for you seeing it every day.

There was confidence in his quiet, she observed. He was sincere and curious, attributes that ought to have stood in contrast to his line-coarsened hands and the lean muscular Y of his body.

Why do you they call you Stray?

My name is Les.

Better, she said.

Over the next few days their small exchanges amplified into a universe of just-missed grazes and glances. She would find herself consumed by the simplest object of obsession: the hairs on the knob of his wrist, his knuckles cradling a cigarette, where the shoulder sloped into the veins of his bicep. Walking herself right up to the knife edge of desire, she would pass behind him after delivering a drink nearby and nearly decide to drag her finger across his bare, sun-soaked back.

Their last day in town was her day off. She wanted to work but found no one to switch shifts.

She went in anyway, late afternoon, pretending to have forgotten her tips the night prior.

John Wayne, pickled from the day's drinking, snored on a lounger.

Les sipped a cocktail.

She crept up beside him, blocking his sun.

You still want to see it through my eyes?

Marlene showed him beaches white as paper, old Victorian inns, whalers' cottages, and carriage houses somehow still standing. The lighthouse and sunken ship, the boardwalk, the hotel where centuries ago presidents stayed. Then a nunnery and a reenactment village, the long-defunct railroad returning to nature, horse ranches and bird havens, making her way farther out of town, where the wild crept in: a golden eagle overhead with a fish in its talons; a coyote hugging the tree line that bordered houses set farther and farther apart; fences disappearing as backyards stretched to fields, farms, orchards. The day bright and luminous.

She stopped the car at her family's property. Wildflowers had recently sprung up across the forty acres her parents leased to a local hay farmer, the vetch like purple islands amid the swirling sea of rye. Nearer to the house the magnolia spread out its old woman's fingers and fragrance. On the land were also several acres of woods stretching back to a wide, bridged canal. Set into the woods was an enormous pond with warped trees winding up out of the water. In winter the entire scene was preserved in ice, as if protecting itself from the cruel wind ripping off the Atlantic. August, mosquitoes infested the banks and the breeze carried up to the centuries-old colonial house the sounds and stink of swamp. Year-round, foghorns bellowed in the distance, the ferries and fishing boats announcing themselves on their way in and out of the inlet.

Marlene told him all of this breathlessly.

How long's it been in the family? he asked.

My parents bought it in the seventies, she said. It was run-down. They fixed it up together. Our lumber company's been passed down in my family from woman to woman for generations, beginning with my great-grandma, who started it with my great grandpa. He died in World War I. She deeded it to my grandma and so on. One day it'll be mine. And then I'm going to build a little house out here.

They sat in silence.

She grazed his hand.

The skin's roughness twisted how she heard her voice in the quiet.

She laughed, insecure.

What's it going to look like? he asked.

I don't know yet.

You got to have some idea.

She did but preferred now to keep it to herself.

Well, then can I come visit?

She softened some, said, Yes.

She gripped his hard hands tightly.

But over that summer Marlene was the one who visited him. The eight-hour drive too much for Les with the quick turn-around between scalloping trips. Before long she had a key to his apartment, arriving early to grocery shop, straighten up, staying after his departure to linger another night in the memory of their sheets.

Captain Alright would sometimes double up trips: ten days out, offload at a different port, a second ten-day run after a night's rest. These occasions Marlene would race hundreds of miles to beat them to ground. They'd rent a motel room, sometimes for just a few hours, sometimes just to lie in each other's arms, Les too exhausted to do much past showering.

Back home in Destiny her mother was full of easy clichés for why Marlene was gone so frequently. She was also never short on criticism for the character of men in Les's profession. But for Marlene there was a vivid clarity behind the logic of her feelings. It was as if she all of a sudden recognized that she'd been wandering most her life and in that realization also understood that she'd grown tired of traveling alone. This troublesome loneliness, which Marlene only just discovered had been with her all along, was at once acknowledged and assuaged.

And then summer ended.

Les split seasons back then, scalloping from March to August and rigging sport fishing boats down in Florida until end of winter. She'd learned of the baby after he'd left. They'd been seeing each other just a few months but she was certain she loved him and rushed to call him.

He took a week to return her messages.

When he finally did, Marlene had been living with such humiliation that she oversalted the happy news with indignation.

He remained silent on the other end of the line.

Are you still there? Say something.

He started, his voice breaking.

Marry me? he said.

She smiled with as much delight as disbelief.

Yes, of course. When are you coming home?

He promised soon.

They made all sorts of plans.

But he stayed gone, invented reasons, claiming to be saving for a down payment on a house.

Marlene's ultimatum came at month four.

I don't care about the money, she said. Besides, you know I want to build a house in Destiny. She had some savings she planned to put to the purpose. Get home or get lost, she told him.

He did neither.

He called more often, left lengthier messages to which Marlene refused to reply. Even so, each time she heard his voice over the answering machine she'd punish herself for believing him, for believing *in* him, knowing this to be some sort of weakness in her, a weakness that felt like strength when it resulted in the quiet conviction to take him back if he kept the one promise she cared about: return in time for the birth, which was exactly what he did.

When the three of them left the hospital, Les pretended to get lost on the way back to his apartment, found himself turned around in a new housing development, looking for an exit. He pulled up to a driveway to reverse directions.

Marlene lost her patience.

She was exhausted, sore, ready to scream.

Angie stirred in the car seat.

He hopped out, grabbed a SOLD sign from the truck bed, drove it into the lawn like a pioneer. Her mood changed in an instant even as her dream of Destiny faded further. She'd never seen Les so handsome, smile so bright. The sun was liquid in the clouds behind him.

Inside, the house was bare but for the nursery: crib, bassinet, changing table and rocking chair, clothes, stuffed animals—the wallpaper a terrifying mural of a giant squid that he claimed *hugged* the room. The next morning the entire crew showed up with their furniture, stocked the pantry and deep freeze. And they left them in peace just as quick.

Les seemed rich in purpose those early months. Angie had her days and nights flipped and Les stayed up eagerly with Marlene, coaxing Angie to sleep, to eat, holding a straw to Marlene's lips, scrawling down weights and diaper consistencies.

One night he sat cross-legged at her feet, rocking Angie, a boyish curiosity in his voice.

I love her so much, he said. Do you think she knows that?

I do.

How does she know?

She knows because of what you're doing right now.

What do you mean?

The way you hold her and talk to her.

How am I holding her?

You know, up high close to your heart and whispering softly into her ear.

I don't think anyone ever did this for me.

She knew not to ask more questions.

She also knew that he'd been hung up on the guilt of missing the pregnancy—that in the instant of Angie's birth, Florida became a shameful vestige from another life, a rebuke of himself he somehow smuggled into this incarnation. She wondered if he thought about scalloping the same way—that he would be leaving them for so long and so often. She wanted to know if his ideas about work had changed now that he had a family.

Have you thought about the job at the lumber company?

Your parents hate me.

You haven't given them reason to feel otherwise.

I said I would think about it.

How am I supposed to run their books?

You'll drive down every couple weeks.

You're not going to leave us again, are you?

He looked up from Angie.

No, never. Why would you say that?

The hurt in his voice was not quite raw enough.

As she suspected, the crew started coming around again not long after.

The warring sides of Les and Stray began to play out intimately before her.

Over eggs, early in the second month, Angie finally down after a sleepless night, she caught him looking at her like a cornered animal.

Another time he came back from a night out with the boys, accusing her of asking him to betray the life he'd been brought up to lead, swearing he'd decline anything handed to him, yelling that he sure as hell wasn't going to work for her.

We'd work together, she replied.

The following week he bared his teeth at the baby when she wouldn't take a bottle.

At the three-month mark he told Marlene he was going back out.

You know how my dad died, he said the night before leaving. I'd never forgive myself if something bad like that happened again out there and I wasn't on the boat to stop it.

What if it happens to you?

The crew needs me.

And like that, Les was gone again.

Out the hospital window, she watches a car swerve into the parking lot and come to a halt beneath the emergency awning. A reed-thin man steps out of the driver's seat, walks around the back end of his vehicle. At the passenger side he opens the door. A woman climbs out, kicks him away as he tries to help. Marlene expects to see her waddle full-bellied up to the sliding glass. Instead she comes out shivering, jacketless, with a flat stomach and flat chest—the most recent girl from The Villas—her mini-dress spangled with sequins, clear heals glinting against the snow. She cradles a wounded hand. The man puts his bony finger in her face, says something restrained, his manner like a suppressed firearm. He jabs his finger into her eye. She cries out, covers her face, yelps again as the injured hand falls. She then follows him through the sliding doors, a pace behind.

Marlene lifts the magazine, trying to remain hidden.

The security guard meets them at the entrance.

Are you OK? he asks.

They walk past him, ignoring his question, and approach the nurses' station, where the man collects a clipboard and forms. They find a seat near the TV.

The security guard persists: Ma'am, are you all right?

She ignores the question again, her good hand supporting the injured one, a nasty cut across three or four fingers. She asks the person next to her what program they're watching.

Ma'am, are you hurt? Did he hurt you?

She holds her silence, eyes glued to the television.

The man she is with never once lifts his attention from the paperwork.

Marlene recalls him from The Villas too. His black hair cut short and cowlicked. Eyebrows sloping, also black. Slightly cocked eyes under reading glasses that tilt on the tip of his nose. She knows him by the straight long strides of his regular patrol from the entrance to The Villas up to the enclosure. The way the tucked tee and tactical pants drape off of his trunk. Bill, she surmises, a man capable of just a few whiskers on his chin and a hopeless little mustache. Aside from the pen, his only movement is a double blink he can't seem to control.

The security guard turns away.

The girl flips him the bird.

He walks to the nurses' station, picks up the phone to call for help.

At that the girl is out of her seat, marching to the desk, screaming.

You fake fucking cop! Leave us alone, you fake fucking cop!

He sets the phone down. I'm just trying to . . .

Fuck you, you fake fucking cop.

The security guard places a calming hand on her shoulder.

Get off me, she says, turning to address the waiting room. You saw, didn't you? You all saw? You saw him just grab me, right?

She stops her tirade cold.

A change comes over her.

She's seen Marlene.

The security guard follows her eyes.

The hush draws Bill's attention from the clipboard too.

He turns to the girl, then to Marlene.

He lifts his reading glasses to his forehead, does that sharp tweak of a double blink again.

There's recognition in his eyes.

A quick, shrill laugh comes up out of Marlene.

She rises to her feet and walks to the exit.

Once through the sliding doors, her step quickens to a sprint.

In the car she pulls a cigarette from a fresh pack, strikes frantically at a matchbook.

The heads refuse to catch.

FOR SEVERAL NIGHTS she refuses to leave the apartment, forgoing her drives entirely. She stays up until dawn distractedly reading the newspaper, folding laundry, scrubbing the oven. Bill knows her, everyone at The Villas knows her, talks about her. The wound that keeps her returning there was a topic among them, her want to care for those women thrown into relief.

What hell was she doing? How'd she let it go this far?

The first time she arrived at The Villas was by accident. She was out on one of her drives this past summer and found herself pointed inland until the bright Vegas-like sign suddenly rose in the night. She knew the neighborhood by reputation but never had a reason to visit. She parked, quietly observed the comings and goings of the SUVs and vans, suburban dads and husbands driving the two or more hours from the affluent townships. Occasionally she even saw police cruisers pull up, cops go inside and come out thirty minutes later. The men she thought disgusting while the girls Marlene envied for their perpetual self-reinvention. They were chameleons, even if each adaptation was at the behest of a different creep.

Marlene's mind turns next to the girl from The Villas. She kindles a low-burning contempt for her, for her pattern of interference, the chattiness at the apartment and now her hospital dramatics. But she also worries if the girl's OK. Something about Bill unsettles Marlene, his easy ominous silence.

She coughs, the oven cleaner fumes irritating her eyes.

She will do something normal for once, she decides.

She will go pick up more scouring pads, leave the apartment to air out.

She puts on her jacket and grabs the keys.

She doesn't need to go anywhere special tonight.

She doesn't need to drive to The Villas.

She will not drive to The Villas.

She promises herself that she will never again drive to The Villas.

She drives to The Villas.

When she sees the girl in the enclosure, hand bandaged, Marlene sighs with relief and annoyance. She lights a cigarette and waits for the next shift change.

The sky open and the wind up.

Trees nodding like a congregation in prayer.

An hour later the new group of girls emerges from the lobby, among them a fresh face Marlene doesn't recognize, one of the few remaining. As she nears the bus stop, the girl with the bandaged hand refuses to leave. Marlene cracks her window. She hears the noises of argument in the air. The fresh face stomps back to the lobby. Marlene continues to watch, sensing the glances cast her way. Bill exits The Villas a moment later. Marlene drops down in her seat. He marches out to the bus stop and drags the girl with the bandaged hand back to the motel by her good arm.

Marlene dabs out her smoke, starts the engine, shifts into drive.

She waits for them to cross the threshold into the lobby.

But the girl breaks from his grip just short of the entrance, Bill continuing inside.

She stands bewildered against the brick façade before turning around to face Marlene's car.

She raises her bandaged hand to wave.

Marlene feels once again ripped from the cover of darkness.

She knows she can't just kill the engine and continue to wait. She won't pull a U-turn, either, headlights off until she completes the about-face. The girl remains against the brick wall, hand raised as if an offering, as if a plea, as Marlene rolls forward to the enclosure, scoops up the fresh face, and drives off.

FIVE

They stop at the top of the Ferris wheel, last go-around. The night balmy, late in summer. Along the pier below are bright carnival lights, sounds of people on rides, laughing, screaming, hollering, the bangs and dings and pops of games won and lost. He is seated across from his girls, the two of them giggling. His daughter holds up the stuffed dolphin he prized for her at the ball toss. Behind his girls he notices something shifting in the air. Look, he says. One pier over, a roller coaster stands out against the night, the train paused atop the first peak, while just above the track hundreds of seagulls flitter like loose paper in the wind. The tide way out, the beaches wide and bare. Far beyond in the distance, lightning cleaves down over the sea. Giddy for the birds, his daughter dances Dolphy, pretending it can fly. Lightning again. Les turns to the breeze to smell for rain, closes his eyes in search of thunder. He senses neither. As if the storm were a baleful backdrop in a theater for the deaf.

Give it here, he says to his daughter, taken by alarm, Give me Dolphy.

Les doesn't know why he asks for it, only that it's critical he retrieve the toy at once.

She ignores him, entranced by the boardwalk bulbs reflected in Dolphy's glass eyes.

Lightning cleaves down over the sea again.

Give Dolphy to Daddy.

He reaches for the stuffed animal.

She yelps, buries her head in her mom's arms.

Hand it here now, he says, his voice approaching real dread.

The lightning behind them quickens, nears.

It skips over the sea like fingers across a tabletop.

He lunges for Dolphy.

The Ferris wheel jolts, his stomach rising from freefall—and Les wakes in darkness.

By the heave of the boat, he can tell the seas are rough.

The bow lifts and crashes and his stomach goes weightless again.

The alarm clock reads 1:27 A.M. Half hour until his watch.

He climbs out of bed, careful not to wake China. The other bunk is vacant, John Wayne already hours into his own watch. Les collects his things by the light of a keychain flashlight. They hit four hundred bags just before he went to bed. Another shift, maybe two, before their steam home.

Outside the cabin the galley is empty, all quiet.

He unwraps the cellophane smothered with Neosporin from his hands, throws it in the garbage. His fingertips are cracked, nails splitting, worked raw by salt water and sediment that seep into the rubber cutting gloves. His skin drinks up antibiotic cream. The method Marlene's. She was always resourceful, ritual in her care of his hands. At home she used to wash them, soak them, moisturize them, massage them back into a relaxed, functional state. Now he spreads his fingers against the wall, presses hard and applies weight, flattening his palms and digits as fully as they allow. Overnight his right hand locked into a ball, the result of clutching a knife for hours on end. His left a talon from palming shells. Then he moves into a hamstring stretch, feels the charley horse coming, and calls the fucker forth, grinning as the spasm takes hold and passes.

He pours coffee into a paper cup and nukes it, chugs a bottle of water.

Next: he uses the head, where he undresses, pisses, resting his forearm against the wall.

He turns to observe himself in the mirror.

His hair is coarse, widow-peaked, buzzed. Eyebrows like caterpillars over eyes seeming to wander closer together with age. His body tall, toned, muscles wiry and roped in veins. His is an athlete's physique, though the closest he ever got to athletics growing up was rigging bait for a sport fishing boat with John Wayne. Weekends and summers Les and his best friend angled on day trips out to the canyons, prepping rods for silky-handed city men who displayed their trophies proudly over bar tops and billiard tables. Les's mom left before he turned one. His dad raised him alone, forbidding the boy extracurriculars and expecting him to earn instead. The old man was pleased with himself when referring to the money his son surrendered as GOLF, Gift of Life Fund.

Les was asleep in his bunk, the rest of the crew, too, when his father died on a steam home years back. Captain Alright sent the old man to bed after he passed out in the wheelhouse. But he must have gone back out on deck instead and slipped over the rail. Nobody knew until the next day. His body was never found. Les's recollections of him are easy enough to call up: the sudden rants and rampages, the almost proud ignorance of the sounds and smells emitting from his body, the slick-backed charm of a man who kept everyone, especially his son, at a jab's distance. What he remembers of his mother comes from a single afternoon when he was four. She'd won a cruise through an office job, called up Les's father out of the blue to invite him. They agreed she'd take a Greyhound in to meet her son before the trip, keeping it a secret from Les until they arrived at the mall. But he knew something was up that morning when his father dressed him in a little sailor's outfit, stooping down to a knee to comb his hair. Les was glued to his mom the whole afternoon, holding her hand, leaning into her thigh as she tousled his hair, sitting on her lap in a photo booth.

His mom never returned after the cruise.

It wasn't exactly a honeymoon was all his father said.

Les stripped his vocal cords when the photo booth reel went missing from his dresser.

It had been nighttime like this when the old man disappeared. Plus winter. Plus pain pills. Plus he was a mean cuss. But no one deserved to drift off into all that dark and all that cold and all that fear all by himself.

Les scans his torso in the mirror, gaze drawn down to where his stomach hair no longer obscures the advance of the bruise across his abdomen. He allows himself to think of his mom, to feel as a child in her presence once more, recalling what it was like to have discovered touch that day. He flushes the toilet, turns on the shower, soaks his head underneath. At the sink he works a squirt of soap into a lather, spreads it over his stubble, scrapes a day's worth of growth from his face. His look is softer shaven. After his daughter's birth he started using a razor regularly, even on the boat a fifty-hour steam from land, even still.

He dresses for the cold: two sets of long johns, two sets of sweatpants, four wool socks, a thermal undershirt, two sweat-shirts, waterproof overalls, and a slicker.

He moves out to the galley to slide on his rubber boots.

The boat jolts, slows. The dredges are coming up.

He wraps his fingertips with athletic tape, grabs his lukewarm coffee and smokes, opens the galley door, and steps out to the covered shucking room on deck: The engine calms to a groaning idle. The boom cranks up the steel scoop dredges from the ocean floor. Wet lines shriek as they thread the pullies, the tremble from the tension vibrating throughout the boat. Booby, running the wheel while Alright sleeps, issues commands over the intercom. The satellite radio blares classic rock. Fluorescent lights flicker and buzz. John Wayne cuts, beard hanging down to where his belly pushes out. The skim of his knife rasps against each scallop. The shells he flings back smack the aluminum chute with a thunderous clap.

Ain't it a fine . . . , Les starts.

Don't say it's a fine morning or I'll shoot ya. McLintock!, 1963.

This was their morning greeting since high school.

Les looks out from the hatch onto the open deck where the overhead lamp holds back the night, lighting the boat bright as a film set. Rain sweeps in from the side. Swell high, waves crest the ice-slicked bulwark with each sway of the boat.

Hoover and Monk, hooded and wet, pull on cupped cigarettes.

Les lights two Merits, puts one in John Wayne's mouth.

Can you believe that? John Wayne says. Kathleen told me to take the damn thing back. Said I was spoiling the kid. Course I didn't. Not my fault she makes making her look bad so damn easy.

What did you get Ethan again?

Smoke less weed, Stray.

It's early.

No, it's late.

A toy car, right?

No, you son of a bitch, a '87 Camaro.

You bought your five-year-old a Camaro? You fixin' it up with him?

Fuck no, that kitten purrs.

Are you crazy? Where you going to put it until he's old enough to drive?

Leave it in his mom's garage.

And let it sit?

Hell yes, let it sit. Park it right next to her rust trap. He's your godson, Stray. You should be happy for him. You should be happy for me too. I'm a single Pringle, baby. You're coming, aren't you? You and Marlene? To my housewarming this weekend? Well, more like renovation warming. New place is all fixed up.

The mention of Marlene and she's with him again.

We'll be there, he says.

Les remains in the hatch while the draggers swing on. He hears Booby call out to Hoover to check a hitch in his dredge. Hoover looks, then shouts for fire. Monk Man uncoils the hose, brings out the welding torch. He observes as Hoover cuts through a joint with the short blue flame, stars spraying from the metal, and fastens the gap with an anchor shackle and wrench. Booby lifts the dredges again, spilling out the catch.

How's the kid holding up? Les asks.

He's slowing down, John Wayne says. Legs about to give out.

What's Alright say?

Booby's call. Personnel's his jurisdiction. He says he's going to work him until he drops.

Everybody still leaning into him?

Like you said, the kid needs to be serious.

You shouldn't have slapped him.

And what about respect?

How's anybody supposed to respect *him* now?

The boat shifts into gear, gains speed, the dredges back overboard, dropping into the depths.

Hoover sorts the portside pile. Monk Man works through the starboard haul. Les drags his cigarette, sips his coffee, watches Monk Man grimace and fuss in pain. He still has not figured out the right way of picking. The kid punches his quads, implores himself to tough it out. Every few seconds he holds the rail for support or stands for quick relief.

Get your hands off the rail, Booby booms over the intercom.

Monk Man moves his hand from the rail. He stands to rest his burning muscles.

Get your nose back in that pile, Booby yells.

Monk Man squats again.

Hoover races through his pile, then jumps to Monk Man's, saying, How are your legs, boy? Like matchsticks about to spark? What'd you imagine? That this was going to be fun? Is that what you thought? That we do this shit for a good time? Then he does his best Booby impersonation: That's some weak-ass TONC shit. This is work. It ain't day care, Dildo Breath.

You should show him how to pick, Les tells John Wayne.

That'll ruin my credibility.

You're the one who hit him.

Exactly. Besides, you love to play the hero.

Is that right?

Yessir—I'm more of a gunslinging sage.

Les spits out his cigarette from laughter.

What? John Wayne says. I can't argue with my nature.

Do I rub your belly for my fortune?

This ain't no wise man's belly. John Wayne pats his stomach. This here's my dickydo.

Your dickydo?

It's what you call it when your tummy hangs out further than your dicky do.

Les shakes his head, turns back to deck.

Monk Man works furiously throughout Hoover's berating, not once reaching for the rail, not once grimacing or glancing up from the pile. He stays focused on the job, desperate to impress the crew around him. Hoover bends at the knees, taunts the kid for his poor form. Does it hurt? Looks like it hurts. Hoover then steals a line from Les's dad: That's *your* pain, man.

Monk stands straight from the agony.

He arcs his back and spreads his arms, eyes turned upward.

I quit, he howls.

He rips off his gloves, flings them overboard.

You watching this? Les asks John Wayne.

I'm watching for that cape of yours to come out.

Fine, I'll do it. I'll show the kid.

There he is—Stray to the rescue!

Les makes a move out to deck.

The bow lifts in the swell, drops down hard.

Booby calls out to hang on.

Les grabs the hatch, Hoover the rail.

John Wayne squats, lowers his center of gravity.

Everyone safe but Monk.

A wave crashes over the bulwark, smacks him in the side, knocks him to the ground, and sends him flying across deck, belly up, limbs straight and stiff, a skate fish trapped beneath him. Les watches the port-to-starboard slide, amused initially by the absurdity of the scene, by this eccentric pioneer of some new sea sport, until on the other side of the deck the kid's legs shoot through a scupper, waist and chest, too, arms catching the opening, halting himself abruptly, just short of being spat into the sea.

Les races toward Monk, grabs him under the armpits, pulls him back on deck.

John Wayne and Hoover there too.

Get the fuck off of me! Monk yells.

Les can't bear to let the kid let go. He holds Monk from behind, hands clasped across his chest, the two of them just lying there, bathed in fluorescence, the rain sweeping over them. A sharp rise in Les's stomach and the dream returns: The more he pleads with his daughter to hear him, for her to find his voice and seek out his face, to hand over Dolphy this instant, the more she remains hidden in her mother's arms, until Marlene's eyes turn to him with pitiless judgment.

He is alone in the distance of her stare.

Monk begins to laugh maniacally, shouting, Yeehah.

Les yips with him, the crew, too, their stunned voices turning rowdy, alive in the dread of having nearly lost one of their own.

SIX

From the kitchen three days later, Marlene watches Les roll over on the couch, waking from an eighteen-hour stretch of sleep. He groans as he sits himself upright, lifts his shirt, appears to examine his stomach, prodding his abdomen, and groans again. He stands slowly, turns, and notices her, pulling his shirt low. She pretends not to spot his limp, the way his body moves hesitantly, hurting everywhere, as he makes his way to the coffeepot.

There was a time when they would have met Les at Lutz's. A time when, after he called home to let them know the crew had returned ashore, she and Angie would hop in the car and hustle to the boatyard, Angie sprinting to the dock only to then retreat at the sight of her father covered in blood and guts and grime. It was their routine: Les gave chase, Angie shrieked, caution from Marlene, *Tetanus* her nickname for the boat. Outgoing, too, they'd sit in the parking lot and watch Les prep, capture every last glimpse of him until he disappeared to sea for weeks at a time.

Yesterday, hiding in her car down the block, Marlene waited for Les to pull up in his truck and tiredly climb the external stairwell to their apartment. She didn't want to be at home when he returned. Her cell phone rang and rang when he called from Lutz's.

She finally answered. Hello?

We just finished packing out, he told her. Leaving here in twenty.

I have errands to run. Probably won't be home.

She hung up.

A half hour later he walked through the front door to an empty apartment.

Marlene sat in her car a short while longer, just enough time to let him dump his trash bag of fish-stink laundry into the washer, shower, and crash, knowing how quickly he would nod off, and for how long.

What relieved her when she went upstairs was his foresight to avoid their bedroom entirely.

He pours himself a coffee, sits down at the table.

She slides him his repair kit.

Advil, Band-Aids, Neosporin, Nivea, plastic gloves, nail clipper and file, tweezers.

Marlene continues through today's newspaper, lingering again on a red-winged blackbird follow-up she's almost memorized this morning. Winter came late, the article reported, which confused the timing of their migration. Hit hard by snow while fleeing south, their tiny overworked hearts gave out in mid-flight. The photo this time is of four birds perched on a power line.

Les grabs an apple from the bowl.

The fruit slips his grip, thuds on the wood.

He tries again.

The apple falls a second time.

Third try he uses both swollen hands, lifts the fruit to his mouth as if cupping water.

Marlene stands, comes back to the table with a knife, slices the apple for him.

He eats as quietly as possible and sips his coffee.

He reaches across the table for her soft pack, pulls the ashtray to the center.

They both light Merits.

She senses his hopelessness, knowing that he thinks she blames him for everything. But an apology from him—more than one, really—is appropriate, and it ought to originate someplace within him that he can't betray. *I'm sorry* is not just an obligatory gesture. It's not a sustained commitment to evolve over the course of a lifetime either. An apology is a willful instantaneous act of trans-formation if only he felt it powerfully enough. After all, down to brass tacks: What was the origin of this fight? Right, he chose to party with his buddies rather than sit down to a meal with his wife. Mistake-remorse, mistake-remorse, was the up-down of the carousel on which his life, not hers, has always spun round and round.

Les finishes his smoke, hobbles to the bathroom and closes the door, turns on the shower.

Marlene sets down the newspaper, chewing a fingernail.

She dabs out her cigarette.

Just across the table where Les was sitting, she sees a folded piece of paper, her name written in his hand. That was once Marlene's move: hiding love notes in his tackle box or in the *TV Guide*. A word or two Sharpied onto a Ziploc of scallops he brought home from the boat, on which he was already scrawling a date and weight anyhow, was the kind of simple, staggering delight she'd always hoped to pull from the freezer.

She opens the paper: *Dinner tonight?*

★   ★   ★

THEY ARRIVE AT the restaurant together though they spent the day apart. Les swung by Hoover's to use the table saw, borrow a nail gun. The replacement door for their bedroom he bought first thing and already affixed to the hinges, but the trim he purchased was too long. He let himself into Hoover's through the side entrance, the house freezing, heat off. He found Hoover in the garage, sanding a piece of wood he'd cut to look like a squirrel, to his side a hollowed pen casing and several lines of powder Les knew were pulverized pain pills, Tupperware over the top to keep free of sawdust. Monk was there, a sway to him, as if slow dancing to music only he could hear.

Hoover lifted the cutout to show Les, then pointed to the wall where two dozen other flat wooden squirrels hung. Shooting trespassers was an exercise of his liberty, he liked to boast, memorializing them in his woodshop as a tribute to their creator. His eyes grew big as he lifted his arms to the sky in silent exultation. He pulled a beer from the cooler, wedged the cutout's front legs and chin over the cap, popped the top with the squirrel.

It's 9:00 A.M. somewhere, he said, offering Les a beer.

Les shook him off.

Hoover handed the beer to Monk instead, who slugged the bottle.

At least have a recreational opiate, Hoover said.

How long you been at it?

We have a baby, Stray. Hoover gestured to Monk. Come celebrate. He's one of us now.

No, thanks, Les said, nodding hello to Monk.

Monk pretended to suck his thumb.

Is he not talking to me? Les asked.

He's been mute since we ran out of blow.

Les used the table saw fast and fled with the nail gain.

Back home, Marlene was gone. She returned to the apartment a few hours later, short of the groceries she stepped out to grab. She motioned him out of the doorway, drew the blinds, laid down for a nap, wine on her breath as she slipped by him. He woke her in time for their date.

At the restaurant the hostess seats them in the back.

They order drinks.

Marlene scans a menu; Les looks out the window.

Bows of trawlers glow in the floodlights, the sterns draped in night.

Snow falls brightly on the docks.

Isn't this nice? he says.

She looks at him blankly.

You see the door? He says. I'll paint it tomorrow.

She looks at him again, nods this time, returns to her menu.

It's Saturday, Marlene. I'm gone again Monday.

You know I don't like it when you use my name, Leslie.

I just want to get along this stay. What's it you say? Find a lifeline.

Do you have any recollection of how things ended last time?

This was two weeks ago. Why are we talking about two weeks ago?

What's two weeks or ten years got to do with it?

Maybe we could get along, I'm saying. What do you think?

What do you think I think?

That's the kind of question that always gets me in trouble.

That's the kind of answer I used to find charming.

I'm sorry about two weeks ago.

Rule of threes, she says.

He takes a deep breath.

I'm sorry about two weeks ago.

Two.

I'm sorry about two weeks ago.

I don't believe you.

He nearly bangs the table.

Please, he says, red-faced. I'll be a fucking Boy Scout.

The waiter delivers their drinks.

Les's head is in his hands and Marlene asks for more time.

His knuckles throb, shoulder clicks, back in and out of cramps. The bruise on his stomach is soaked deep into the muscle. She must know how hard it was for him to repair the door in his condition. And now he's just said sorry. The demand for apologies throughout their marriage, the constant parading of them, has tattered those shopworn words. Of course, she'd scoff at that notion too. She beats everyone to moral high ground, in every relationship, with an opportunistic certainty about the right way of living. Still, he tries to call up the thing that needs saying, to hand her the win he knows she's after. But how she can be any crueler, he can't comprehend.

Did you just say *a fucking Boy Scout*? she asks. Is that what you said?

Yes, I said *a fucking Boy Scout*. What's wrong with saying that? What did I do now?

I mean, it just sounds close to *Boy Scout fucking*, I guess.

He looks at her confused.

She smiles.

Like, someone fucking a Boy Scout? he plays along.

Yeah, like that. Or like you fucking a Boy Scout.

No, no, no, I *am* a fucking Boy Scout.

Oh, I get it. Yeah, makes sense now.

I don't fuck Boy Scouts.

Thanks for clearing that up.

They return to their menus.

Marlene breaks the silence a second later.

Well, actually, wait. If you didn't mean that you fuck Boy Scouts, or someone fucks Boy Scouts, then do you mean like the image of a Boy Scout who fucks? Or, like, a Boy Scout in the act of fucking? Like *fucking* as an adjective. A battering ram. Running water. A fucking Boy Scout.

Jesus, no, I'm not making any commentary about the sex lives of Boy Scouts.

OK, good, that's a big relief.

You sound like one of the crew.

Are you trying to hurt my feelings?

It's a joke they would make.

I guess I know my audience, then, she says.

I'm aiming for a Best Behavior badge is all I meant.

I like your sticking with the metaphor. But Best Behavior badge is not a thing.

Sure, it's a thing.

Not a thing.

It's a thing. But whatever, you just watch. I'm going to impress you this weekend.

I'll believe it when I see it.

You'll be watching, huh? You like watching? Watching fucking Boy Scouts?

Too far.

Got it, too far. My mistake, ma'am.

Don't call me ma'am.

My mistake, Marlene.

She smiles again.

Now you're definitely sleeping on the couch tonight.

The joy on Les's face dims and Marlene looks away.

They eat their meal, order dish by dish, the banter slowing, conversation turning general. The evening stretches out and they relax into a cautious rhythm. They remark upon the people, the food, the view from the window, avoiding anything heavy for once. Marlene, with a few glasses of wine, eases some, and then appears to ease some more, amused, she admits, by how many ways Les can rephrase the question How are you? Between courses they rise together, step out for cigarettes. Each visit the snowfall redraws the parking lot with a simpler geometry. Les tries to not betray his disappointment over Marlene's remark about sleeping on the couch. He's grown accustomed when home to waking in the night, staring at the ceiling for hours, craving the exhaustion he finds at sea, which puts him down unburdened as the dead. A brush of his foot against her ankle, the back of his hand flush with her thigh, the pulse in her neck like a hypnotic timepiece—he would never admit that these are his only relief from an unstill mind.

THE NEXT MORNING begins much the same. Marlene makes coffee in the kitchen, reads the paper, anxieties quieted by a hidden sun, by the drab winter light falling through the slats in the blinds. Les wakes on the couch where he slept alone, the full soreness of his body arrived, Marlene observes, as he again lifts his shirt and prods his stomach.

After a brief silent stay at the kitchen table, he announces that he's off to Lutz's to prep for tomorrow morning's departure. Then he'll be home to paint the door before John Wayne's party. Is there anything you need help with today? he asks.

Let me think about it.

Maybe we could do it together. Whatever it is.

OK, she says, nodding.

Les leaves.

Marlene stays out all day.

She's forgotten the resolve required to go along in daylight. With Les home, she needs to interact in plain view, conjure the vigor most folks faked to maintain the appearance of a full life. She preferred to grocery shop in the middle of the night, but yesterday, it was a run to the supermarket she decided would help her pass for diurnal. As soon as she entered—the arresting fluorescent lights, the vaguely familiar clerks, the last lone shopping cart at the end of the corral—she backed out of the sliding doors before they closed behind her. The fear that small talk could atrophy from disuse stole her breath away. In her car she asked her thoughts to quiet, to quit. A few storefronts over was a broke down bowling alley with a pool hall in the basement that still served. She ordered a wine. Tomorrow will be better, she told herself. She went home to nap. Les was there, blocking the entrance to the bedroom, nail gun firing.

Today she returns to the shopping center and struggles to enter the grocery store again. A woman pulls up next to her, gets out, walks toward the store. Marlene musters the nerve to follow her. Once inside the supermarket, though, she can't let her go. She tails the stranger from aisle to aisle, grabbing all the same items, until the colorful array of cereal boxes sends her mind reeling and she abandons her twin shopping cart.

She finds her way back to drinking wine at the pool hall.

This time more than just a quick one.

She buys a second bottle from the bartender, stumbles to the beach.

The angry ocean gray, the sky gray, but for a wedge of blue where the clouds fall short of the horizon. Marlene's mind wanders to the girl from The Villas, the ice cream growl and her raised wounded hand, the man poking her in the eye. She sits among the dunes, fingers buried in snow down to sand. They spread Angie's remains on a beach not far from here. The wind scalded her face that day, as today. The water was similar, too, hundreds of whitecaps peeking open like eyelids across the sea.

They show up empty-handed to the party after dark.

Marlene's drunk.

She doesn't want to be here, has bones to pick with most of the room.

She hugs China first, holds him tight, sidestepping Booby with her back to him. She asks about Cynthia, and China says his wife is home watching the twins. Les then introduces Marlene to Monk Man, who does not speak. After an awkward silence, his girlfriend tries to introduce herself but Marlene interrupts before she can get her name out, telling her it's a waste of time until she proves lasting. Like Janny, Marlene jokes, Booby's *newest* fiancée. Marlene takes hold of Janny's hand, shows off the ring she appraises at *not less than $20K*. Next, she brings up the new trucks out in the cul-de-sac and the renovations inside John Wayne's house and the boat purchases present company were no doubt planning for the weather change. She turns to the two women to make her ultimate point. Save it while they make it, she says. We might be in the pink right now but their bodies break down. If they live long enough to enjoy that.

Price of scallops won't be up forever, China agrees.

We can thank your people for that, can't we? Booby says.

I'm not taking your shit tonight, old man.

Please, not tonight, Booby, Marlene pleads.

The earthquake in China five years ago, I'm saying. Doubled our price per pound.

The tsunami was in Japan, China says. And the undertow destroyed the seabeds all the way across the Pacific. The shit messed up a lot of fishing back home in California. Destroyed peoples' livelihoods. For good, maybe. My sister says my pops can't even find a spot on a dragger anymore. Damage was so bad, they still won't let them bottom trawl.

That's my point, Booby says, looking to Janny. We can afford it.

Where were you and Hoover today? Les asks Monk.

Monk stands there, rocking back and forth, teeth grinding, wiping his palms on his jeans.

Another long pause before his girlfriend nudges him.

You and Hoover still getting after it? Les says. That why you skipped prep?

Knock it off, Booby says. Kid had a rough first go.

What did you do to make easier?

More than you and JW.

Since when can new guys miss work? Les goes on. Since when can Hoover?

He has a point, Booby, China says.

Booby glares quick and cross at China.

Then he turns back to Les.

Stop talking your shit about my nephew, Stray.

Stray, Marlene says. A nickname any wife would wish for her husband.

There's a hard knock on the door, then it swings open.

Kathleen enters, holding Ethan.

John Wayne marches to the entrance to intercept them.

He wants his father, she says, setting down their son. You deal with him.

I told you I was having a party tonight.

Well, I got a date.

She jerks her arm free of John Wayne's grip as they both step outside.

Ethan stands in the quiet room, noises of an argument coming through the door.

He sees Les and walks over.

Hey there, little man, Les says, pulling him in close.

Marlene and Les share a sad smile.

John Wayne comes back inside, incensed.

He swoops Ethan upstairs.

When he returns, he approaches Les and Marlene in the kitchen, Hoover there too.

He pours them all shots.

Welcome to my disaster of a housewarming, he says.

Disaster of a renovation warming, Hoover corrects him.

Disaster of a renovation warming.

They take down their drinks.

What happened? Marlene asks.

Kathleen dropped the kid off is what happened, Hoover answers for John Wayne. This poor dick was just trying to have a good time, show off the reno, this fucking kitchen, that fucking wall, this fucking paint, that shiny-ass tile, let everybody know that all his new digs are slicker than cat shit. All this poor dick wanted was to show off his fucking this and his fucking that and these fucking cabinets, you know? Hoover turns to the cabinets. Jesus, look at these beautiful cabinets, all white and glossy. Like, really. They're amazing fucking cabinets. I'm not messing with you. He opens one, growing more excited. There's new shit in there too. Look at this, look at that, look at this, look at that. Who's Kathleen on a date with? you should be asking.

Hoover's soaked in sweat.

I swear, if you wake up my boy . . . , John Wayne warns.

How about a quote, JW? Marlene suggests, pouring herself another drink. Something about being a man. No, no, never mind, not that. Anything but that, really. Let's do something sweet, please. Did the Duke ever say anything about being sweet?

Or sad? No, not sad. You crybabies are always pretending not to be sad. Or better yet, something about being a man. That's it: the philosophy of it all, she says, lowering her voice to sound gruff.

God-damn, I'm the stuff men are made of! John Wayne tries.

Marlene laughs so hard, she spits a sip of wine onto John Wayne's new floor.

Hoover, finding Marlene's hysterics contagious, also spits out some of his beer.

Come on, he did not say that, Marlene replies. Who says shit like that? Try again.

Never apologize, mister, it's a sign of weakness.

Anticipating her response, Hoover laughs louder than Marlene.

You don't believe that, right? Marlene asks, wiping tears from her eyes. Like, you don't take these quotes serious, do you? Not apologizing? What kind of women do you all date? OK, OK, never mind, rule of threes. She winks at Les.

He gives a final attempt. *Tomorrow is the most important thing in life. Comes in to us at midnight very clean. It's perfect when it arrives and it puts itself in our hands. It hopes we've learned something from yesterday.*

Hoover bends at the waist, comes back up squealing.

He takes a lap around the kitchen island, howling and shaking his head.

His voice dies down when he sees Marlene standing there grinning.

Her thoughts float buoyantly in John Wayne's words.

She kisses him on the cheek.

You've always been a surprise, she says.

Ethan is heard crying upstairs.

Dammit, Hoover, John Wayne says. You maniac!

John Wayne shoves past Hoover, who slips.

He scrambles to his feet, starts cussing up the stairs where John Wayne disappeared.

Quiet but for the boy calling for his daddy.

THE SCREEN DOOR claps shut. Les has Hoover outside to cool him off. Hoover opens a mini Ziploc, dips in a cigarette butt, brings the smoke to his mouth. You want some booger sugar? he asks. Les says no, lights Hoover's cigarette, then his own. They smoke without speaking. Hoover gags, bends over to throw up, retches bile and stands again, fills his lungs with the cold clean air.

You good? Les asks.

Good.

You're not going to do anything stupid, are you?

No, I'm not.

I brought you out here to tell you not to do anything stupid.

I'm good, man.

Just take it easy, please.

We're grown-ass men.

The two of them stand in the yard and take a leak.

Overhead, the sky is a deep gloomy green.

Great white clouds merge in slow herds, their collisions muted and soft.

Les hears a break in Hoover's stream and looks over.

He's no longer peeing on the snow but urinating on his hands.

What the fuck are you doing?

Nothing, man. What do you mean?

Look where you're pissing, Hoover.

Yeah, I know.

What the hell you pissing on your hands for?

Dude, my heart is a fucking freight train.

Hoover starts hopping up and down, dancing, straddle-legged, one foot then the other. His laughter rising. He zips up his fly, half dries his hands on his jeans, and flees to the front door, giddy as hell. Les calls after him to stop, finishes as fast as he can, runs inside.

Hoover's back in the kitchen, apologizing. He shakes John Wayne's hand, grasps hold of the back of his neck, makes a show of getting along. Les then sees the crown of a head just above the kitchen island. It's Ethan. Hoover bends down to say something to the kid. His hand tousles the child's hair, pinches his cheek. He offers him a potato chip.

The boy's eyes turn up to his dad for permission.

Les loses himself to rage.

He senses Marlene looking his direction and he finds her eyes. She's watched the anger come over him and Les sees her claim a measure of his fury as her own. There's an understanding between them just now as he marches across the living room, his strides aimed for Hoover. A step away she grabs Ethan, picks him up, and turns him to the wall. Les brings his forehead down on Hoover's nose. The crack of cartilage echoes louder than the screams and a spray of blood wallpapers the new cabinets, a scattered-poppy pattern.

HOME, HE NURSES his own cut. They're at the kitchen table, Les working from Marlene's vanity mirror. She watches him concentrate. The skin split just to the side of his widow's peak will make a handsome scar one day, she thinks, imagining another woman years from now admiring it, asking about it, finding the story heroic. He and Marlene are long divorced in this scenario, which somehow heightens the moment, imbues it with a sense of urgency and sadness, makes her want to imprint herself onto his memory, if only as a conscientious edit during the retelling. She stands, hovers over him, the fog of wine and cigarettes on her breath. He leans back from the mirror, reads her desires. Their lips meet, tongues attempt to fasten, to knot. She climbs onto his lap, takes off her top, and goes to remove his shirt.

He pulls it back down.

She tries again.

He grabs her wrist.

Don't, he says.

The mood changes in an instant.

She's already off his lap, marching to their bedroom.

Please, Les calls after her. We're steaming out in the morning.

Marlene kicks a hole in the baseboard of the new door and slams it shut.

Run back to your other family, she yells.

She stands at her bedroom window, listening to him collect his laundry from the dryer, toss it into a fresh trash bag, and leave, closing the front door softly behind him.

SEVEN

M arlene guides the girl's hand down onto the kitchen table, removes the splint, unwraps the Ace bandage. She cuts through the gauze, shuddering as a view of the wound opens. The middle three fingers, broken just below the knuckles, are distended, bruised. Sutures sprout from the pool of color. Her pinky is the most horrific: swollen to the size of her thumb, the tip black and bulbous. The girl's hand, free of support, shakes unsteadily on the table. She keeps her chin up. Her eyes move between Marlene and her fingers, her fingers and Marlene, and on occasion to the broken door, this one different: kicked in, not rammed through.

Marlene plunges a rag into the bowl of soapy water and rings out the excess. She wipes each finger, working around the sutures and lifting the dried blood crusted beneath them. She saves the pinky for last, washing the tip as if polishing a scrap of some black glass artifact. She dabs the skin with antibiotic cream, wraps the hand with fresh gauze, reapplies the bandage and brace, covering it all with a plastic grocery bag she ties off at the forearm. She leads her to the bathroom—a towel, nightgown, and hanger stacked neatly inside, as before.

Earlier, Marlene swung by Lutz's to make sure Les's boat had left for sea.

Then she parked down the street from The Villas.

The girl snuck up behind the car and jumped into the backseat.

What the hell are you doing? Marlene said, reeling from the scare.

I'm breaking the fourth wall. You know that term? *Fourth wall?* the girl asked. I took theater in school. It's like the space between the audience and the stage. And you're kind of the audience—right?—out here watching us. And we're definitely the actors. I'd say some of us might even deserve an award—not like a Oscar or anything, but maybe a Golden Globe or a Emmy? Anyway, this, what I'm doing now, this is breaking the fourth wall. She went on to tell Marlene that the reason for the intrusion was that there weren't any more new girls for Marlene to take home. You plowed through us all, the girl said. Besides, I'm starving.

Well, I ain't a chauffeur, Marlene told her, slapping the seat beside her.

Well, I ain't nameless, the girl said, hopping into shotgun.

Her name was Josie and Marlene made her a feast to match the last.

She eats as hungrily as before, eats everything down to the nib, but slower with the use of only one hand. Marlene looks on, smoking cigarettes until she finishes. She clears the table and puts on the kettle, pulls a fresh carton of ice cream from the freezer, and sits down beside the girl.

Marlene scoops out a bite, raises the spoon to Josie's mouth.

So, she says, what happened to your hand?

That ain't the same door, is it?

Did the man at the hospital do that? The one from The Villas? Bill.

It's a new door, am I right? Was that your husband?

That was me, again.

Temper, temper.

It was an accident.

So was this, Josie says, raising her hand.

She opens her mouth for another spoonful.

We have this one client. Guy's a real jerk. The other day he wanted a girl over. Nobody volunteered, of course. It's my job to decide who goes. See, Bill and me, we've been together a long time. Many lives, he says, but who can't count past this one? He says mine is the only soul he's ever met that's older than his. He says they were both lit by ancient fires. It's why he calls me Josie, instead of Josephine. For the Steely Dan song. He calls you Deacon, says you got the Deacon Blues. Still, I raised hell the entire drive over to this creep's house. Trying to talk Bill out of it while also trying to talk this girl I brought into it. I told him none of us should have to go in for this guy. Somehow it took me all the way to the front door holding her hand before I had this gut reaction, like, *No, fuck that*. I turned right around and just walked us back to the car. I tried opening the door. Bill tried keeping it shut. I pried it open enough to slip my fingers in. Then *thud*. The door bounced off my fingers like they were made of rubber. He didn't mean to do it. He'd never hurt me on purpose.

What about when he poked you in the eye?

Poked me in the eye?

Yes.

He never poked me in the eye.

I saw it, honey. So did the security guard.

No, no, no, that never happened. You saw wrong.

You were right outside the hospital.

You're not exactly a role model, you know? I mean, I see you judging. And how do you think that's OK? How can you do that with a straight face? My grandmother was like that. Kind. Quiet. Judgmental. She should've talked more about herself. I'm the opposite, you probably guessed. I've always thought that sharing intimacies is the best way to get on the good side of people. Even if they don't show me at my best. I used to play a game with her, trying to get my grandma to tell me about her life. I called the game Me-You. I'd start by volunteering something about myself and then it would be her turn. Why don't we try? I just told you about Bill and my grandma. Tell me something about yourself. Me. Now you.

Like what?

Could be anything at all. Small stuff. Or big. Then we'll be on the right side of each other.

Marlene blurts out the first honest thing that comes to mind.

I hate this town.

OK, I guess that counts. Where else would you go?

She waits for Marlene to say more.

Marlene says nothing.

I don't hate this town at all. Bill and me lived out of a car for years. Hungry and cold a lot, but we were together. There was power in that. Like no one could harm us against our will. Still, you find yourself pulled to places. Desperation is kind of a magnet. That's how we found The Villas. We crashed a few nights and learned that the owner was also hurting for money. Most of the rooms were already being used for the same purpose. We were tired of moving, tired of bathing in creeks and shoplifting. I made new friends and we cut the old man in. The Villas is the only home I've ever had that's my own, you know? Where'd you grow up?

Destiny.

Fancy.

Our house wasn't in the rich part.

I'm guessing there's no poor part.

I thought you wanted me to share.

You're right. Sorry. What's Destiny like?

Marlene doesn't want to tell Josie about the house down there that's now abandoned, her parents leaving it unoccupied and moving to Florida after Angie passed. Or the drag-out fight during which she said all the right things to make sure they stayed gone for good. She decides to lighten the mood, looking around the room for something inconsequential to impart. She sees the door again. She wants to defend Les, to say something forgiving about him. How he used to laugh in his sleep, for example. Awakened in the night, Marlene would lie there smiling to herself, grateful to share her life with a man who could dream so joyfully. Angie was another story altogether. She snored like a drunk, the noise reaching every corner of the house, sometimes waking Les and Marlene both. They listened in bed together, giggled about their booze-crazed toddler watering down bottles in the liquor cabinet and the surprise in store for a future lover. She misses the sounds of sleep in her home, the soft rise and fall of an even breath, the nearby dreams and heat of a body at rest. But she doesn't want to share this either.

She grabs a piece of bread from the basket, takes a bite, chews, and swallows.

A moment later she hiccups.

Then she hiccups again.

And again.

Room temperature bread gives me hiccups, she says.

Josie's eyes light up. Bread gives you hiccups?

When it's room temperature.

You're messing, Josie says.

I swear, Marlene says. If it's warm or buttered, it doesn't happen.

Marlene hiccups a fourth time, a fifth.

Josie shakes her head in astonishment, smiling.

Works, doesn't it? she says. We're on the good side of each other now, aren't we?

Yes. We are. Me. Now you.

Josie bolts from her chair, picks up one of her clear spiked-heel shoes from the ground, fastens her good hand into the straps. I was also a tumbler in school, she says. Holding her injured hand close to her body, she leans to her right side, presses the shoe to the ground, kicks her legs up in the air, completing a cartwheel. She goes back the other way, silly with laughter.

Stop, Marlene says, voice raised. Please stop.

Josie ignores her.

You're going to hurt yourself.

Josie keeps at it, back and forth, the heel clicking against the floor each time.

You're going to hurt that hand again.

Marlene feels the air in her lungs drawn from her. Her chest heaves, collapses. The room withdraws. The walls, the girl, the table—all pull away like the ebb of a tide. Angie, four, Dolphy in hand, donning Nana's nicest heels and dress, plodding out to the backyard in Destiny, where she proceeds to march in straight precise lines up and down the lawn, digging her heels deep into the grass with each step, a serious-about-business look on her face.

Les is out scalloping. Marlene drove down to collect some documents.

Pop watches from afar before riding his mower over.

Nana comes out of the house to observe.

The day velvet, autumn.

Angie continues her walk across the lawn, digging her grand-mother's high heels into the damp earth with every step, the tail of the dress now caked with mud.

What in the world is she doing? Pop asks.

Aerating the lawn, Nana answers.

Hell she doing that for?

You never give Nana a reason to wear her nice things, Angie says. So I invented one.

They laugh so hard, they gasp for air.

Josie drops back down to her feet, giggling, takes a rest on the floor. Her eyes roll to Marlene, who's stunned still, her mouth screwed up sideways, hiccups jolting her body like electrical currents. Marlene fingers her wet cheeks, tries to say something, to pull a sound up out of her throat. Something like: I've done it. Am doing it. Can still. Cry.

THAT NIGHT MARLENE dreams that she's walking across the property in Destiny. Hay season over, the ravaged field sprawls brown and gruff with stubble. The cloud cover, complete just moments ago, tears open. Sunlight pours from a rip in the sky, kindles the fall-patched trees to the west, paints Marlene's cheek, the forgotten touch of warmth wondrous. Overhead, a flock of birds shift in the sky. At the tail, two fall behind, wheeling, lost at play. The first climbs higher and the second nearly catches up before they both turn to dive, cutting sharply through the air. Near ground, one vanishes behind the tree line and the second opens its wings and rises. There's a moment when Marlene fears that the first bird will not return. There is a moment, as the second bird hovers where the first disappeared, when sunlight clips its wing and shows it red.

EIGHT

S tripped young of the illusion that the world has been conquered, charted, angled for human need, Les has always preferred the scale of life at sea. Out here bait balls the size of football fields appear from nowhere, the water surface suddenly sparkling with tens of thousands of glinting fish. Biblical weather arrives full of portent. On clear days, when the faint curve of the planet is the only delineation of sky and sea, thoughts warp toward the terrors of myth. Les might imagine a skyscraper tsunami lifting out of the horizon. Or in the inscrutable white of fog, the waters haunted and the hazy sun a second moon, the boat might steam into the open mouth of an awakened leviathan. At dark, as now, the net mesh of stars slung low from the corners of night, the crew asleep but for Alright in the wheelhouse and Les in a camping chair near the stern, surf rod in hand, Les finds comfort looking out at the faraway lights of other trawlers, ten or twelve spattered across the distance, like prospecting camps in the heart of the Atlantic.

They left yesterday on a fifty-hour steam and have another fifteen or so before they drop the drags. Everyone on board ignored Les, speculating under their breaths about his motive for brutalizing Hoover. Hoover's decision to remain in his bunk belowdecks was therefore understood. Monk Man, too, stayed out of sight in the same cabin. When the two of them skipped prep—the first day spent on gear work and reinforcing the twine and steel circles of the dredges—Les, China, and John Wayne grew angry with Booby, who refused to intervene as first mate and uncle.

John Wayne also stayed away from his old friend, which was fine by Les. A few years back, Les witnessed John Wayne empty two clips into a shark that attacked their long lines. He popped off fifteen rounds, slipped the mag, loaded another from his coveralls, racked the chamber, the shark diving by then, and proceeded to squeeze the trigger again, all within a few efficient seconds. John Wayne's tendency to overreact gave Les misgivings about telling his friend the truth. Les kept to himself instead, embracing the home of his routine: burning off the turtle guards with the welding torch; spray-painting the dumping bars, red for port and green for starboard; tying blue pieces of rope to the cables at 80, 100, 120 fathoms.

As expected, he replayed the last night with Marlene, ashamed that even when he shined his own best lights the marriage still dimmed with failures of understanding and kindness. He knows he doesn't possess the excess of courage needed for endings. Men rarely do. And his mind turned to a desire to hold her, to know the relief of having earned acceptance in this life.

Your godson's scared of you, John Wayne said later, coming up behind him.

Something heavy rolled over inside of Les at the thought of frightening a child.

He told John Wayne to sit, deciding to volunteer one detail. Having slept on board the night before they left, Les observed everybody arrive at the boatyard. Last to show was Hoover, who stayed in his truck until the fuel had been pumped and ice stored and the groceries were unpacked before he snuck belowdecks undetected. He got out once during the hours-long wait, Les confided in a hush. He climbed into another car for a quick second. Then he grabbed his bag from his own truck and made his way down the dock.

That's bad news, John Wayne said. Alright needs to know.

It'll tear the boat apart.

Booby, then? He's sorted Hoover in the past.

I tried once already.

Before or after you broke Hoover's face?

Before.

Why'd you do it?

Les ignored the question.

OK, then, you and Marlene fighting again? That why you slept on board?

He ignored that question too.

Les hears a noise fifty yards off starboard. A black shape rises from the pearly water. A great back rolls into view and vanishes. The whale swims somewhere beneath the boat, and beyond the groan of the engine and the voices over Alright's VHF radio Les becomes aware of a vast silence. He grins, lights a Merit. The ocean makes him feel small, and when alone, and at night, gratitude reliably follows this feeling of smallness. Moments later, portside, the water bursts. The enormous back slides up once more and disappears. Les throws his feet up on the rail, lets out some line and adjusts the drag, pretends to rustle the constellations with his rod tip.

THE NEXT DAY the first shift begins without sign of Hoover or Monk. Tension over the matter persists while shucking in the box. John Wayne cuts with his violent splashing rhythm, the hollow one-two percussion of each flung shell against the aluminum chute meant to alert Booby to his irritation. In retaliation, when China asks John Wayne for help lifting his basket up to the trough, Booby lashes out at him, sparing him no insult. China drags his basket to a scupper, shucks from there instead. For the next several hours Booby and China pick baskets on the same side, sorting the port haul together. They race to the middle, China always winning, Booby throwing shadow punches each time their paths near.

Les witnesses all this from his station. He presses shells into his stomach, each shiver of pain a shock before he numbs to the wound. He flicks the innards to the sea, listens to the hungry cries of the swooping gulls, watches the boat's wake disperse back into the long memory of the ocean.

A terrible noise issues from the engine room.

The boat decelerates, the wake dying.

Les almost tumbles over his cutting trough, stomach slamming hard into the ledge.

Then silence.

A seagull barks and dives for the knife that slipped Les's grip and fell into the water.

The boat lists from side to side before it levels, calm again, drifting tamely to starboard.

Les runs down to the engine room to assess the damage. He knows right off that the steering column snapped, the chain and master link ripped in two, dangling on the floor. He scours the engine room before searching the gear locker for spares, removing and returning the immersion suits and safety harnesses. Next, he goes outside to the lazarette, a large storage compartment near the stern beside Les's cutting station. Nothing there either. Les kicks himself for not double checking for extra parts while they were onshore, even if it was Hoover's responsibility. He climbs up to the wheelhouse. Booby is already there.

We got no steering, Les reports.

No shit, Captain says. Details, alright?

Chain snapped. No spare.

There goes money! Alright yells, slamming down on the armrests of his captain's chair. Two of everything, alright? You got to have two of everything. There's no AutoZone out here. Who the hell was supposed to load parts for the engine room?

Hoover, Les replies.

He came straight here from the hospital, Booby says.

Yeah, but he missed a prep day on land too, Les says.

Alright shakes his head in anger.

You'd be off my boat if I didn't know you from the time you were little, Stray. We don't put hands on our own. We protect each other, alright? I thought you knew that. Shit, of all of them, I thought you were the one I could trust to know that. Alright stews for several seconds. Lutz ain't going to be happy diverting a second boat just to tow our asses home. But, shit, the steering column's probably his fault anyway. Using Band-Aids to stitch this old bitch. He addresses Booby. Weather tracker says we're clear, thank the Christ. Raise the draggers and drop anchor. And you, Stray, I'm blaming you for this. You're going to make it up to me somehow. You'll make it up to the whole crew. I want eyes on the water, you hear? The whole time, alright? Keep your ass glued to that deck, you understand? Nod to me you understand. Les nods. If the winds start blowing and the swell rises, we'll be up shit's creek with our dicks for paddles.

THE SUN ROLLS lazily across the horizon, dragging dusk along behind. The pale gray sky marbles with lavender and orange, the sea no longer blue but a glittering mineral black. For hours Les stares out at the ocean and for hours the water sends back slight and terrible phantasms: Shadows galvanize to the east; the wind quickens over his skin; whitecaps clone in the swell. Les both perceives these details and doesn't. They're anchored in a restless ocean, that much is certain.

He sits in a camping chair portside. John Wayne, starboard, trims a mattress pad down to the size of his berth, tosses the excess foam overboard. China rests on a bucket nearby as they share a pipe, stoned. China's been sorting scallops by color and condition—violet, bone, brown, orange-pink, large and small, striped, chipped, and barnacled. He now arranges them next to each other, five, then fifty, a hundred, more, as if solving a puzzle he is instantaneously devising. The crew abandoned the scallops on deck after the steering blew, the hard work to cut not worth the price for such a pitiful haul. The three of them are talking about how to handle Hoover and Monk.

Telling Alright will split the crew like a log, Les says.

What if we're rotted already? John Wayne says.

If you tell Alright, you'll make a bigger mess, China says. He'll side with Booby. Then it's us in the crosshairs. Me more than you all, I bet. It's pretty clear where loyalties lie.

What should we do? Les asks.

Seems to me we're screwed either way, China replies. Hoover and Monk fucked up our money this ride. Telling Alright will mean Booby's bound to fuck up our money next ride.

All Stray cares about is harmony on this boat, John Wayne says.

It's a good instinct, China says. But I'm here for the paycheck, no disrespect.

They load another bowl, pass the pipe around, quiet again.

You know what struck me first about Kathleen? John Wayne says.

Since teenagers Les has known John Wayne to be a reflective high.

What's that? Les asks.

Her teeth.

Her teeth?

Yeah, her teeth.

What is she, a horse?

This was back when Sebastian was still alive.

Sebastian was his pet lobster, Les tells China.

I've heard.

I used to take him around on a leash, John Wayne says. This one night I went to the C-View with him for a quick one—he was the best little bar-top companion—and a woman started chatting me up. She had this big toothy grin and Sebastian seemed to take a shine to her. We wound up talking most the night and then at one point she stood, put two quarters down next to my Bud, and said to give her a call. I joked with her that people used cell phones nowadays. She smiled big, those huge beautiful teeth, like real chompers, and she said that I'd skipped the step of asking for her number. She walked away without giving me the chance. Shit, was I charmed! I went back every night until I saw her again. John Wayne, grinning, stops talking. She's not fighting me for custody. She and her new boyfriend plan to just skip town. How am I supposed to explain to a child that his mom doesn't want him? Shit, I'm sorry, Stray, John Wayne says, backpedaling. I'm not really asking you that.

Les knows it's an innocent question, but a few silent answers come to mind: Don't rename the kid's mom something horrid. Don't burn and bury all memory of her existence. Don't drink until dawn, drug daily, and make questions about her acts of sedition.

What made Marlene stick to your ribs? John Wayne asks.

You're taking a tour of all my favorite subjects.

I was with you in Destiny. You two flipped like switches. She's beautiful, smart. She's a good heart. I always liked you two together.

E: All of the above.

Fine, then how'd you propose? That line you used.

You remember how it goes.

Hell yes, I remember. But it's a good story.

Tell it again, China agrees.

Les gives the short version: I was down in Florida working on a sport fishing boat and she called me to tell me she was pregnant. We'd only dated a few months but she wanted me to come home. She was, like, *Les, shit or get off the pot.* And I was, like, *Well, my dear, in those terms . . .* John Wayne and China both deliver the line with him: *I guess I'll shit.*

The three of them laugh.

What about you, China? Les asks.

How'd I get engaged? Like you, I got Cynthia knocked up. But twins. So we got married.

You all met out here on the East Coast?

She grew up here. I came out for art school. That's when we met.

Art school? No shit?

I lost my tuition money to the top end of a straight flush.

That's a bad beat, John Wayne says.

I've had a few of those. I lost our dog to Cyn's brother on a football game last year. The dumb shit gave me even odds on a ten-point spread. But then my quarterback broke his ankle. The bastard collected too. I couldn't believe it. He made me march the dog down the driveway while my boys were staring at us through the window, and then he just pulled away. Their uncle didn't have the balls to come inside and look his nephews in the eyes. Honestly, it was bad, but the bright side was Cyn was more pissed at him than me. The tuition money was different, though. No forgiving that. My dad's a hard man. He grew up in a little fishing village in Vietnam, fought in the war, and then fled across the world with nothing—no money, no English, no family—all before twenty-five. He won't talk to me anymore. I send money to my sister. She helps out my parents. They got nothing since the bottom-trawling ban.

I'd quit after a beat like that, John Wayne says.

I'm building my bankroll back up.

I don't understand how you can still gamble.

I don't understand how you can afford not to.

It's good you got fishing to fall back on, Les says.

It feeds the mouths in my home, China says. That's all it's good for.

I did three semesters of college, John Wayne says. Football scholarship.

I never went to college, Les says. Debt's like a prison sentence.

So's scalloping, China says.

They all agree.

Booby steps out on deck and pisses through a scupper.

Hey, Booby, John Wayne says, those tweakers still holed up down there?

Real subtle, Les says.

Fuck your face, JW.

You going to do anything about them? John Wayne asks.

Stray wrecked Hoover's nose. And you, you angry ape, you smacked Monk.

Somebody's going to get hurt out here, Les says.

Somebody did get hurt.

You hired Monk, China says. And Hoover's your blood.

You telling me how to do my job, China?

I'm just saying that you're the only one who can fix it.

You got all of these ideas, little man, so tell me, please, how should I handle it?

How about imagine one of them was me. Let's go down there and drag those fucking TONCs out of their room, China mocks him.

Booby zips up and starts on China.

You even know what *TONC* stands for?

I don't want to know.

Temporarily outside native country. It's an abbreviation.

That's an acronym.

Booby stands over China, who remains seated on the bucket arranging scallops.

It's also the sound the skull makes when border jumpers get popped by ICE. He addresses Les and John Wayne now. You know boys, I been doing this job for ages. When I first started, it used to be the Portuguese TONCs out here, then the Russian TONCs, now we are working with Chinese TONCs, and before long Mexico TONCs will be driving wages to hell.

Jesus, you're dumb, Booby, China says.

Don't take the Lord's name in vain.

I'm from San Jose.

Where are your parents from?

Where are *your* parents from?

Don't be a smart-ass. Where are they from?

Nope.

Fine, don't answer. It doesn't even matter. You don't have to be Chinese to be a TONC. And you are definitely a TONC, China. No, he says, quieting John Wayne and Les when they try to interrupt. I'm making a point. You know who here's not a TONC, little man? Stray is not a TONC. He's an asshole, and he's got some big fucking emotional problems, but not a TONC. John Wayne, also an asshole, also not a TONC. Alright ain't a TONC neither. Hoover and Monk right now are TONCs, but that's a temporary designation. But do you know why you're a TONC, China? Look at those arms on you. They got no meat on them at all. You can hardly lift a full basket on your own, and by the end of the haul you're too run-down to carry your load. We got to do our job plus yours, meaning you're not pulling your weight. Meaning you have this job instead of someone who can do it the right way, and that, China, makes you a TONC. Permanent. You're fixing to be the next one I replace.

China's eyes blaze.

I got your attention now, I see, Booby says, laughing. Look at him, he's fuming. He can't even hear the word. Say it. Say the word. Say *TONC*. Go on. Say the word and you'll stop being one. That's the rule. Ain't that the rule, boys?

I swear to God, Booby, Les says. You better stop.

Say it, Booby says to China. Say the word and you become one of us.

Cut the shit, John Wayne says.

Fuck, look at the way he squats over them scallops. Stray, if your dad were here . . .

Fuck you, Booby. And fuck my old man.

What was that? Booby staggers back. He doesn't know what to do with himself. He starts to say something and stops. Well, I'll be having a chat with Alright about you three boys, you can goddamn count on that. And none of you better dare come after my nephew.

Take it easy, Booby, China says with great effort.

Take it easy, my ass! You're off this rig, little man.

You don't want to do that.

Look at you, telling me how to do my job again.

I just don't want to have to tell Alright how bad your arthritis really is.

I ain't the slowest cutter, Booby says, rubbing his knuckles.

Yes you are, Les says.

By far, John Wayne agrees.

You can barely hold a cigarette in your hands, China says.

Booby starts for China, who ducks him.

What the hell is going on down there? Alright yells.

He's come out from the wheelhouse to check on the commotion.

Well?

They all hesitate.

Jesus, Alright exclaims, that's fucking beautiful.

The crew follows his widening eyes down to the scallops China arranged on deck. John Wayne and Les shimmy up the A-frame to get a better look. They hang from the beams just off the flounder nets. Booby looms for a second, standing over China, before hopping up on top of the fishhold. They all peer down from their perches to observe the arrangement of shells, the movement of shape and color transforming into a giant mural of a woman's face in profile, nose lifted bravely to the wind, eyes a piercing green, long waves of hair flowing to starboard. An angry scrape of a shovel across deck as China cuts a line through the center of her face.

From nowhere they hear the blow of a foghorn. Then another. In the near distance the tow steams toward them, lights flashing, crew all out whooping on the bow, pants down to their ankles, hands wagging their dicks in the air. The foghorn blows again like a groggy sea creature's groan.

NINE

Marlene no longer feels compelled to visit the old house, those memories of Angie's first month of life, the tired new parents still fresh with wonderment; or the park nearby where Marlene and Angie chased fireflies at dusk, Marlene finger-painting streaks of luminous guts across both of their cheeks to quiet Angie's anguish over crushing one; or the Shoney's up the highway the three of them went to for breakfast whenever dad was home, Angie insisting on a coffee mug for her juice while Les threw back shot after shot of creamer singles to their daughter's delight. Those drives failed to sooth Marlene for some time, and she sheds them as impassively as skin, bypassing them now for The Villas, preferring Josie's presence to the dimly lit lots of the past.

They are at the kitchen table, Marlene cutting through the gauze on Josie's hand.

Whose turn is it? Marlene says.

Josie doesn't answer.

She's quiet tonight, drawn in.

Everything OK? Marlene asks.

Me, now you.

Fire away.

Have you always been a housewife?

Wow. Shit. Is that . . . am I? That's how you see me? God, I had a very different life in mind. But I guess I've always been a caretaker, that's true. For family, though. I've never really had friends. Why would anyone volunteer for that much theater? Do you like what you do for work?

A heater for a heater.

I mean, do you find it empowering?

Where'd you hear that?

I read it, maybe.

That's stripping. A lot of dancers find it empowering. No one thinks of The Villas like that. Except the money. Beats fishing, from what I can tell. Those men don't age well.

Some don't age at all, Marlene says.

One way or another, everybody sells their body for work. Me, now you.

I collect clippings of those blackbirds that went down last month, she says, after a moment.

You do not.

I know most of the articles by heart.

Did you hear about the horseshoe crabs?

Marlene shakes her head, eyes back on her task.

It's got to be here somewhere, Josie says, opening the newspaper on the table with her free hand. She flips through a few pages, taps a headline to show Marlene. Here it is.

Horseshoe Crabs Spawn Months Early, Confusing Locals,
Scientists

They came up out of the ocean, laying their eggs way before they were supposed to, Josie says. But the awful thing is that the sand was too cold to bury them. So they just left them there. Bill calls it the *tooth and claw*, same with the birds, times when the human shine rubs away and the world becomes just a giant thing eating itself, one town at time, one species, one industry, one mother—she pauses—one child.

Marlene knows she's being pressed for a reaction.

She folds the washrag, dips a corner into the hot water. She cleans around the sutures before following the same path with iodine on a cotton ball she affixed to eyebrow scissors.

You two talk about me?

No.

Sometimes?

It's just that he sees things other people don't. He's got a way of looking at the world.

I wish you wouldn't discuss me.

OK, Josie says. Listen, I can't spend the night.

What do you mean?

Bill wants me back.

Why?

He thinks I'm here too much.

But you're not.

I'm here every night.

What if I talk to him?

It won't matter.

It's still broken, Marlene says, dropping her elbow onto the table.

She hears the desperation in her own voice.

She collects herself, commences to remove Josie's stitches.

She clips a knot and pulls the thread with tweezers.

But the thread keeps slipping her grip.

I don't have to go right now, Josie says.

Marlene nods, continuing to work on the sutures until they're all removed.

As Josie bathes, she remains at the table and reads the article: On a beach several hours south of Destiny, hundreds of horseshoe crabs crawled out from the ocean depths to spawn months earlier than expected. Unable to dig deep enough into the freezing sand, the adults crept back to into the sea as the eggs scattered in the winter winds and waves. The black-and-white image shows the glistening shells stacked on top of each other as far down the beach as the lens could grab, as if countless numbers of combat helmets had washed ashore. Marlene pictures herself out there among them, at high tide and under a full moon. The ocean thrashing nearby. She drags the adults through the sodden sand, tirelessly returning mothers to eggs, only for them to slowly rotate and begin the deliberate crawl back to the black waters.

Marlene, Josie says.

She steps into the living room, done with the bath.

Marlene, she repeats.

Marlene emerges from the sequence of her disturbed dream.

Did they know? she says. The article doesn't say whether or not they knew.

Her voice like a bemused child's.

Josie walks over and touches Marlene's shoulder.

They both turn down to the newspaper.

Marlene doesn't ask her to stay, but Josie spends the night anyway.

MARLENE HAS NEVER spoken to Bill before, never even heard his voice, but she spends the next day in perpetual negotiation with him. She's worked out a simple, persuasive pitch: She's his best customer, Josie's injured, so why should this arrangement need to change? She reminds him that she also has rules to maintain, boundaries she'll not betray. She'll never pull up to the motel and never enter The Villas. Bill will understand, respect her for them. Then he'll make an offer, saying something half-ominous, half-comical, like *Have my little girl home by curfew.* In her head that's always his line. When she arrives at The Villas that night, however, she's astonished to see Josie already in the enclosure. Marlene rolls forward watchfully and Josie climbs into the passenger seat. At the stop sign, Marlene pauses, eyes on the rearview mirror.

Were you in trouble? she asks.

I told him it was an accident and it would never happen again.

And that worked?

No.

There's discomfort in her voice, stiffness in her body.

Marlene decides to skip the gravity of ritual tonight. They cook dinner together, drink wine, chat with the radio on in the background, all while Marlene observes Josie move around the apartment with the same hesitancy as Les when he's back from scalloping. At one point a news story about the horseshoe crabs airs. They quiet down, listen intently. Marlene stirs the saucepan while Josie leans into the counter. Prehistoric creatures that walked beneath the dinosaurs, horseshoe crabs were not crabs at all but more akin to giant fossilized scorpions. They possessed ten eyes, including one on the tail, chewed food with their feet, detected ultraviolet light from the moon, and contained copper in their blue-glowing blood, which was harvested for chemo-therapy. Capable of monitoring the heights of the stars and the depths of the oceans at once, the horseshoe crabs were mystifying creatures, Marlene and Josie agreed. The eggs on the beach had frozen, the report confirmed at the conclusion, but why the adults spawned early was still uncertain.

Josie walks gingerly to the radio to turn the volume down.

They knew, she says. They had to. They're little alien gods. How could they not?

She looks to Marlene for a reaction and Marlene is caught scrutinizing her.

I need to pee, Josie says.

She stays in the bathroom for a while.

She comes out shuffling her feet, distant, drugged. Her pupils pinpoints and constricted.

Her hand performatively high to overemphasize the injury.

She takes a seat on the couch.

Marlene sits next to her.

Why do you stay with Bill?

We saved each other.

What does that mean?

We both had it tough a while back, Josie says, words slurred. His mom left his old man when the meth lab blew up in the woods. Bill was, like, seven.

That's not what I asked.

Josie ignores her.

This was in backcountry PA, but she moved them south. He grew up on a commune in Kentucky. His mom met this evangelist. I don't even like to think about that bastard. He wanted a boy, one of his own. Instead, they had six girls, Josie laughs. One right after the next. She was awful too. His mom. She did nothing to protect him.

Never mind. I don't want hear this.

Every Sunday his stepdad delivered a sermon to the family and every Sunday after that sermon while they were all still gathered, he would beat Bill unconscious in front of them all. One time he cracked him in the forehead with a belt buckle.

The twitch?

Josie's eyes fall heavily, pushed down by the weight of half-moon lids.

I'm guessing you're not staying over, Marlene says.

No staying over.

Like tonight?

Like ever.

Josie sleeps and sleeps.

An hour later, Marlene tries to rouse her.

Then again later.

It's time to go, she says. Bill wants you back. I'll call a cab.

Josie wakes once, eyes open yet still adrift.

Why do you stay with Les? she asks.

She returns to a sleep that lasts until the late hours of morning.

THE FOLLOWING EVENING Marlene remains parked down the street from The Villas with no sign of Josie. There was sun all day. From the shuttered apartment she heard the melt rushing down the gutters, but as she sits in her car the temperature plummets. Glass creeps back up the naked trees. Moons drown beneath the ice of shallow puddles. The longer Marlene waits for Josie, the more concerned she becomes and the more compelled she is to stick around for the next shift change. And the next, and so on, until the hours stretch to dawn, and suddenly, out from The Villas, Bill walks up to the enclosure.

In the streetlight his slim silhouette is striking: lofty, somber, secure.

Marlene observes him speak to the girls.

When he returns to the motel, one of them starts the fifty yards to Marlene's car.

She walks down the center of the road. Her crystal pumps tap the blacktop.

Marlene rolls down the window.

You lonely? the woman asks.

Neither acknowledges the other from a night together months ago.

No, Marlene says.

The girl walks back to the enclosure.

When a second does the same minutes later, Marlene turns her away as well, understanding this to be a game of Bill's, an attempt to shatter her anonymity and scare her away.

To the third Marlene replies boldly.

You remember me? she says. I remember you.

Are you lonely?

Is Josie OK?

Are you lonely?

Tell me if Josie's OK?

Are you lonely?

Fuck off.

Marlene leaves before the fourth girl reaches her car.

This goes on for several nights. From the moment she arrives at The Villas, the girls offer themselves one at a time, relentlessly, Josie still gone. Marlene's days are spent sitting alone in her living room, blinds drawn, ashtray on end table, electric blanket humming on her lap, replaying their last conversation, her push to wake her and to put her in a cab. All while speaking aloud as if Josie were answering back. She then nods off in the early afternoon, awakening at dusk on the verge of panic, mood swinging from exhaustion to dread, before she marshals the resolve to return to The Villas.

On the fifth night she tells one of the girls that she wants to speak with Bill.

The girl walks to the motel, and a half hour later he exits, aimed for her car.

The sudden thrill of fear jolts through Marlene.

She suppresses the urge to flee.

As he nears, Bill holds up his hand, telling her it's OK.

Then, a few paces later, his fingers gesture her to roll the window down.

Deacon, he says. Can I bum a smoke?

She hands him a Merit and a lighter.

Marlene sees his handsome sunken face up close for the first time. But the pop of his lips after each drag, the sloppy way he puts the entire filter into his mouth, appears performative. As if he were unselfconscious about his own sense of menace. His twitchy blink the only exception.

I'll pay double, she says.

She waits for a response.

He seems disgusted by the cigarette.

You hear me? But I want her to be able to spend the night.

He waves the smoke around like a stick of incense.

What is it? she asks.

Huh, what's that? Bill's voice is serene, natural. Listen, I ain't your priest.

Why'd you want a cigarette?

It covers the smell.

What smell?

Your color, Deacon. It's a green, greasy film around you. Sticks to you like motor oil. Plain as day if you got the sense for it.

He clicks his tongue and takes a drag.

You're rotting. Your spirit.

She tries her best to keep an even expression.

Get that rich bitch off your face, he says.

I'm sorry.

Nothing about you is better than me.

I know.

You've no clue how much pain comes through my door, Deacon. How much anger. Men who believe the bad things in their past give them superpowers, their heads nodding all the time, agreeing with some hateful voice inside that nobody else can hear. Living for most isn't like TV. It ain't all sunshine and Shirley Temples. Most people don't get their cherry. You're no different. We've all had things taken from us.

Why are you doing this?

Your color works a spell on Josie.

No overnights, fine. Just let her keep coming over.

I understand why you do this to yourself, he says. The Villas. It makes sense to me. Still, I worry about you. Your husband gone all the time. He's a fisherman, right? Les is his name? Out for a week, sometimes two? And there's you, alone in that apartment. So, sure, you get up at dark and work the night shift with the rest of us. But what surprises me is that you don't see how vulnerable you are here. No one knows you come here, do they? Or what about at home? What if someone tried to hurt you there, Deacon? What if someone broke into your apartment and no one was there to help you. No one to stop it. What a person could do with that much time.

You don't need to threaten me. This doesn't need to end.

Depends on if you got any cartoon pj's Josie hasn't tried on yet.

Why won't you listen to me?

Or a favorite bedtime book maybe you all haven't gotten to.

She's told me things about you too. You're awful to her.

What were you planning for the finale of this dead daughter send-up?

I know you've hurt her. You hurt her the other day.

Your daughter wasn't a goldfish, Deacon.

I know about your stepdad, she says.

He double blinks like he's protecting his eyes from an invisible swarm.

Marlene's suddenly sick with worry, knowing she just betrayed Josie.

I'm sorry, she says. She didn't tell me anything.

There's that rich bitch again, he says.

Please, I'll just swing around to the entrance and pick her up. Let me see her.

You know shit about me, that's what you know. You know shit about Josie too. About us. But let me tell you a story. A love story. It's ink black. But love, still. There's this girl. Her childhood filled with ups and downs, mostly downs. An abusive father, in and out of jail, each time serving longer and longer stretches. A mom too strung out on dope to argue when grandma takes over guardianship. Happy times for our girl when she moves in with granny. She's finally allowed to be a kid. Safe and fed. No longer terrified to go home, no longer living with the fear of what her dad does to her mom as the girl pretends to sleep. This goes on for a few years, these easy times. Joyful, OK?

But then things change. She's beginning high school when beloved granny starts burning dinners and bleaching the darks. Soon the girl comes home every day to find her in the living room, rocking in a chair, a suitcase by her side. Grandma waiting on her dead husband to pick her up for their vacation. At school, things aren't better. Older boys show interest. There's a boyfriend, son of a fisherman that steals his daddy's pain pills. There's *heroin*, he says with scornful emphasis. The girl gets addicted and arrested. Meanwhile a pot roast sets fire to granny's kitchen and our girl is kicked to a lockdown facility for at-risk youth. She tries to hang herself one night, but a counselor, a man ten years older, finds her at lights out with a sheet fastened around her neck.

Cue the romance music, Bill says, because from there on out, whenever this counselor works her unit, the girl sets off a Code Red and needs restraining. Slow, it becomes clear to this guy that the girl's edge is cut only when it's his body pressing down on her, his weight on top. They think about each other all the time. A rabid desire tearing at them both. He takes more shifts in her unit, daydreams for the next time she gets violent with another resident and needs handling, when he's allowed to run his fingers over her budding body again and she can grind against him, sly, not noticed by the others also pinning her down and asking her to contract for safety. Life gets complicated, though. The counselor gets caught up in a tangle and needs to leave town. He goes to work one last night to convince her to come. That night defines them. A pact is made. They run away together, decide to be a home for each other. They never lie and never betray one another. They'll be together always. In this life and the next. Nothing comes between them.

From nowhere his entire body flexes.

The tendons of his neck flare.

He juts out his bottom teeth, rolls his eyeballs back so only the whites show.

His arms drop straight down, curve slightly at the elbows, fingers tensed.

He bends his knees but his back remains straight.

She watches him shake with terrible intensity as he continues that hideous pose.

Stop! Marlene yells. Stop this!

Bill lets up, works his jaw loose of the tension.

That's something the bastard made me do in front of a mirror for hours. He wanted me to see my demon inside—you know, horseplay exorcism.

I don't know what you're talking about.

I want to see you do it.

Marlene can sense the faintly controlled emotion in his voice. Now she can hear his inflexibility. She will never see Josie again. A sorrowful defense grips Marlene: She'd only started coming here as a distraction from her pain. She'd only wanted to be relied on in the face of all that was absent from her life with Les.

Goddammit, Bill snaps, startling Marlene. Show me.

She unfolds her arms, drops her elbows to her inner thighs, unclenches her hands. She opens her mouth, eyes gaping, and lifts her nose to the ceiling, the knob of her head resting on her upper back. Her position more relaxed than Bill's but for the taut fibers of her backward bending neck. It's over, Bills says. Never show up here again. Marlene doesn't want to let go of the pose. She remains poised between actual pain and performed anguish, refusing to give up her silent scream for a real one.

TEN

Drunken towhead cherubs recline on cloud puffs amid a broad blue sky. Adoring women, topless, with togas slipping down their backsides, refill bejeweled goblets. A soaring circle of archways, just beneath the high painted ceiling, frame sculptures of the heroes of myth. Thick marble-looking columns drop to thick marble-looking floors on which gold-looking trim and flameless sconces flicker. Sheet-clad cocktail waitresses take orders with pen and paper. Music thumps from a DJ booth beneath a stretch of sports-tuned TVs. Beyond, the casino hums with slot machine jingles, uproars from roulette hits and blackjack doubles. They lean onto a long, ovular, marble-looking bar, John Wayne half engaged in conversation with the bartender, Les half immersed in video poker. The two of them smoking, awaiting drinks.

The tow home was smooth, the weather cold but not unkind. The days sheathed in fog. The other boat dropped them off at Lutz's forty-eight hours early from their expected return. What their wives would never know was the logic. The crew would play some cards, split a suite, and go home tomorrow. The idea was China's but the rest of them, even Hoover and Monk once they came up from belowdecks, did their level best not to admit the same line of thinking. Everyone caravanned together but Booby and Alright, who both stayed home, wishing them sour luck. The more money they lost, the sounder he slept, Captain crowed. Debt means a resilient, reliable crew.

The bartender sets down their drinks. Her toga gold, makeup glitter also gold.

Poseidon Punch and a Zeus Zinger, she says.

What is this? John Wayne asks. Hazardous waste?

He laughs, eyes the colorful cocktails in delicate stemware.

The bartender looks at him, confused.

My drink is blue. What in the hell do you put in a drink to make it blue?

It's blue for Poseidon. She points to the bearded trident wielder up in an archway before turning to Les. Yours is yellow for Zeus and lightning—

About that, John Wayne interrupts her. He stops himself. Never mind.

Out with it, JW, Les says.

No, never mind.

For crying out loud.

This is supposed to be ancient Rome, right?

The bartender nods.

Well, Poseidon was Greek. So was Zeus.

Again silence.

The Roman names for those two are Neptune and Jupiter.

The bartender stares at him, her mouth parting.

Like Neptune Nectar or Jupiter Juice, am I right?

He grins.

She shakes her head and walks away.

Les turns from his full house to his friend.

What? John Wayne says, defending himself. You don't remember history class?

I remember you leaving a fish to rot in the ceiling tiles, Les says.

That's 'cause the teacher called you dumb.

He called us *both* dumb.

Stray, you grabbed your junk in the middle of class and yelled, Hades nuts!

That was you, JW.

Was it? he asks, trying to remember. Huh? No kidding. A moment later he says, We should've gone to the Wild West bar.

Isn't that a little obvious, John Wayne?

The girls wear spurs. And they serve domestic.

How you prefer women with shit on their heels to Greeks in bedsheets, Les says.

Romans.

Huh?

Romans, you dumb shit.

They laugh, gulp their drinks, and ask for the bill.

Off the escalator, their boots clap against the wooden floor-boards. Frontier town façades adorn the walls: bank, post office, general store, saloon. Murals of pioneers striking gold in the mountains, sifting the glimmering nuggets in the stream. They make their way to the bar, passing table games that take on an outlaw affect. They mount stools overlain with saddles, look up at the twenty-foot rock wall jutting the top liquor shelves, a miniature train whistling through a dynamite tunnel. The bartender tips his cowboy hat.

Shot and a Bud on two, John Wayne says.

They take their shots, order another round, down them too.

Les withdraws into the somber ebb of the booze.

He watches his mind veer to Marlene, knowing this detour well.

He imagines what she'd say about him not going home, knowing in his stomach that this is a kind of betrayal. But he also can't bear returning. Only more fault for him to claim.

What is it now, Pilgrim? Your conscience?

The Man Who Shot Liberty Valance, Les says.

What damage you doing inside yourself right now?

You ever think about how ugly Hoover's life would be without fishing?

Bullshit you were thinking about him.

It'd be hopeless, man. Is that why Booby won't do anything?

I couldn't tell you what Booby's thinking. Truth is I never understood his debt to Hoover.

Nothing is simple with family.

Hoover shot out his eye, Stray.

Booby gave him the damn BB gun in the first place.

Still.

What was Hoover, ten? I remember going over there around that time. Hoover wouldn't come out. He was too busy doing chores—his dad's, his mom's—doing them all before anybody had the chance. He was tireless. This scrawny little thing. Trying to scrub the guilt from his heart. Hell, he was just a kid messing around in the woods. Booby's the one that should've been more careful.

Why'd you hit Hoover, Stray?

'Cause you were about to.

John Wayne laughs.

Was I?

Yes.

Really?

Les nods his head.

Don't suppose you care to elaborate.

No.

OK. Good enough for me.

John Wayne kicks back his beer, finishing it off.

Listen, we should jet. I got to pick Ethan up from my sister's in the morning.

I'm going to stick around awhile longer.

Come on, Stray. Let's go home.

You really think we ought to tell Alright?

Stray.

You say it's got to be Captain who handles this mess, but I'm not so sure.

Stray.

Maybe you're wrong.

Stray, dammit.

What?

Come with me.

No, I'm fine.

What are you doing, man?

What are you talking about?

I don't know. I ain't a therapist.

No shit.

Go home.

This is about Hoover and Monk.

No, it's about you now.

Don't do this.

You know I rushed into things with Kathleen because I was jealous of you and Marlene. Not, like, deep, but surface jealous. I liked the idea of four of us sitting down to eat at a table together. And when four became five, five became six, because I liked the idea of six of us sitting down to eat at table together. Our kids coming up together. Friends like we were.

Please stop.

Let me finish. Kathleen and I didn't fit together so natural as you and Marlene. We were circling a square, she and me. That's all pretty obvious by now. You know, we only fucked sober once? The afternoon when she told me she was running off with another man. It was the greatest sex I ever had in my life. Sober, right? Who knew? Every woman I've ever been with has told me that they preferred a drink or two in me whenever we got groovy. Said I was sweet. Believed I found a rhythm, if you know what I mean. Guess I was too about business without the booze. Except for that once with Kathleen. What's that say about me? What's that say about all of us? About our chances to hold on to something that needs rhythms, caring ones, just to last.

What's your point?

Shut the fuck up, Stray. You're breaking my concentration. I'm flowing here, man. He pauses again, waiting. I'm thinking, OK? I've been thinking, you know? That's what's been on my mind, lately. Wishing I'd put a greater portion of myself into my marriage, wondering if maybe I could've prioritized a little different, thinking how nice it would be to try it sober with Kathleen once or twice more. You see what I'm saying? We don't need you out there, Stray. You pretend like we do. But we don't.

John Wayne waits for Les to respond.

Les takes his time.

I think I prefer the movie quote version of you, he says.

John Wayne laughs sadly, shaking his head.

He puts on his jacket.

You're a persistent cuss, Pilgrim.

John Wayne walks away.

After another shot, Les finds the elevator to the basement.

The doors open.

He exits onto a balcony floor, makes his way to a parapet that looks down over an expansive, symmetrical room built of imperial red timber, flowers carved into the lintels and joists. Hanging from heavy beams, intricately cut wooden wall panels separate poker rooms from the main courtyard where geisha dancers sway to stone chimes at an opium pace. Two gold-painted, tined-tongued dragons swim atop the fluorescent bar. Overhead, a colored glaze roof appears backlit by a fake moon. Also backlit by a fake moon: windows with exquisite appliqué design. Les eyes China at one of the poker tables, sunglasses on despite the dim paper lanterns strewn across the space, enormous jade Buddha pendant hanging over his T-shirt.

Les takes the double staircase, comes up behind China.

Figured I knew where to find you.

Why's that, bro?

You know, the same way John Wayne couldn't sit still anywhere but the Wild West bar.

That's offensive, Stray.

I was right, wasn't I?

Not all Asians gamble.

No, but you do.

Yeah, well, you're still a racist.

No I'm not. China raises his eyes to Les. I am? Like a Booby racist?

No, Stray, not like a Booby racist. But you shouldn't stereotype.

The action comes around again to China.

Rub my lucky Buddha, he says.

Les rubs the jade pendant.

China raises.

Les becomes aware the black chips China's throwing around are five hundreds.

Did John Wayne scoot?

Yeah, Ethan duty. You want to grab a drink?

I don't drink when I play.

So, take a break.

What do you want, Stray?

Nothing, I guess.

You need someone to worry about, why don't you go check in on Hoover and Monk?

They getting after it?

Talk about stereotypes. China tells him the room number, hands Les the keycard. Go see for yourself.

Are you coming up later?

Nah, bro, China says, shutting Les out with a grin. You know where to find me.

Upstairs, Les knocks before scanning the key card. The lights are off inside, terrace doors open. A cold calm breeze carries a mist into the suite. The radio plays from somewhere in the unlit room. Les pulls from a whiskey bottle he finds on a table. He carries it with him to the balcony. He looks down to the rain-slick boardwalk, to the silence falling from streetlamps, to the moon's reflection in the high tide of the wetlands as though an orb floating beneath the marsh grass. He hears the sigh of tires somewhere beyond, then noise from the bathroom. A light underneath the door, giggling. He locks up the terrace and walks over. In the dry tub Hoover sits with a girl: big hair, leather pants, fur coat. On the floor, Monk is asleep by the toilet seat, a petite girl, mini-dress with too-tight ponytail, passed out at his feet, belts around both of their arms, needles on the tile.

Stray! Hoover proclaims. We're having a Narcan party.

The girl in the tub laughs.

Not a stir from the others.

Les kicks away a pair of clear high-heeled shoes blocking the door.

He sits on the sink top, bottle in hand.

He lights two cigarettes, hands one to Hoover. What's a Narcan party?

It's when you take turns overdosing and then reviving each other, the girl answers.

Complimentary with every purchase, Hoover says, tossing him a bottle of the nasal spray.

It's not a real thing, the girl clarifies. Narcan parties. We're just joking.

Hoover turns to the girl in the tub, points to the medical dressing on his face.

He did this to me, he says, nodding to Les.

Don't tattle, she says.

After a moment she sits up, climbs onto his lap. He puts his hands on her hips. Her body twitches and he withdraws them. She removes the gauze beneath his nostrils, then peels the bandage from the bridge of his nose. She looks deep into the bruises around his eyes, the popped capillaries, the cut where the cartilage collapsed. She seems lost for several seconds before she takes off her coat—shirt, too—and lifts her arm. Above her bra sit three scars lined up like a tally.

Hoover reaches to touch them.

She slaps away his hand.

Your turn, she tells Les.

No.

Yes, Hoover agrees. Take off your pants.

No.

Your shirt, then.

No.

OK. Your pants.

The girl laughs again.

She climbs out of the bathtub, steps over Monk and the other girl. She bends down and unzips her friend's minidress. The girl out cold, limbs heavy. She slips an arm through the shoulder strap. Look, she says. She removes a bandage from the girl's ribs. Seven scars this time, the two at the bottom fresh and inflamed.

Her look lingers on Les like a question.

He slugs the bottle, sets his Merit on the edge of the sink.

He strips off his jacket, lifts his shirt, and reveals what remains of the bruise across his stomach, now edged green and sallow.

Damn, Stray!

The girl approaches Les and touches his stomach.

She runs her nails through his body hair.

The tingling running down his spine reminds him how many years it's been since someone other than Marlene has touched him. It feels too good; he grows embarrassed. Then she does too. The three of them look at one another—each marred distinctly by scabs and contusions and scars—and before anyone can find a word to say, the girl's eyes fill up with sudden delight.

You hear that? she says. It's your song. That's your song, Josie. Wake up. Your song.

She runs out of the room in a hurry, turns the radio loud.

Hoover stumbles from the bathtub, falls on Monk and the girl.

Monk groans.

Fuck you. Get up. We're dancing, Hoover says.

In the living room the girl high-steps in her heels like a stilt walker.

She circles the carpet. Her body splashing.

We're gonna break out the hats and hooters / When Josie comes home

Get up Josie, your song. Come dance.

Hoover follows her around the circle, doing the rooster with his busted face.

We're gonna rev up the motor scooters / When Josie comes home to stay / We're going to park in the street / Sleep on the beach and make it / Throw down the jam 'til the girls say when

Get up, Josie. We're dancing.

She about-faces. Hoover does, too, the girl now following him.

Lay down the law and break it when Josie comes home

Les looks on, amused, thinking: Now here's a story.

From the bathroom Monk Man stumbles.

He tries to say something to Les.

The music is too loud.

What?

Monk says it again.

And again Les says, What?

She's not fucking breathing, man! he screams.

They rush to the bathroom.

Her body splays on the tile, head torqued against the base of the toilet.

Les reaches her first, checks her pulse.

I can't feel anything, he says.

He puts his head to her chest, maybe the faintest beat, but he can't be sure.

Call an ambulance.

No fucking way, Monk says. They'll bust us if they find our shit.

And if they find a dead body?

The girl runs to her phone.

Don't give them the room number, Monk tells her.

Les grabs the Narcan from the sink top, rips it open. He fastens the nasal cone to the plastic tube, uncaps the dose, recalling his commercial fishing safety training.

The vial shatters in his hand. He gripped it too tight.

Fuck, fuck, you got another? Tell me you got another.

Monk freezes in the doorway; Hoover disappears.

He returns with another box, tosses it to Les—too high and fast.

Les reaches up, pulls it from the air like a fleeting prayer, a grim silence as he and Hoover glare at each other. Les handles the nasal spray with care this time, twists the vial into place until it locks. He shoots the dose up her nostril.

They wait.

Nothing.

Hoover paces, goes to look for a third dose.

Monk Man remains in the doorway, hands in his hair, pulling at his face.

The song blares from the other room.

Les doubts himself, double-checks the instructions.

His heart sinks.

He was supposed to shoot half the dose up one nostril, half up the other.

He pleads silently with the girl. Please, I'm sorry. Wake up.

Then aloud: Please, wake up, please, please. I'm sorry. I'm sorry.

He doesn't think he can bear any more guilt.

She opens her eyes with great effort. Her eyelids the battle-field between worlds.

She's the raw flame, the live wire

Her mouth parts and chest rises.

She prays like a Roman, with her eyes on fire

She mutters something.

Les puts his ear to her mouth.

Her whisper what floats up of a drowned cry.

My song, she says.

ELEVEN

As usual, Les calls Marlene from Lutz's when he picks up his truck the next morning. He helped the two girls down to the lobby to wait for the ambulance, left Monk and Hoover holed up in the suite, sweating the emergency vehicles. He went looking for China, found him grinding away at a blackjack table. He made the decision then to take the long cab ride to the boatyard alone and he exited the casino with first light in the sky.

He charges his cell phone in the truck, leaves a message for Marlene.

Hey. Just back. En route home.

To support the lie, he throws on his filthy fishing clothes and shaves in the bathroom before driving to the apartment. Entering the complex, he sees Marlene's car parked a few buildings away from their own. Then, looking closer, he notices her figure slumped down in the front seat, watching. His exhaustion sinks to hopelessness. It's been their habit so long, this distance they inflict on each other, and he knows it started with him. He parks in front of their building, climbs the perimeter stairwell, one hand holding a trash bag, the other heaving himself up by the rail.

He's still awake when she walks through the front door an hour later.

On the couch, washed in daylight from the blinds he raised, hair wet from the shower.

You're awake? she says, falling back into the door. Why are you still awake?

I saw you in your car when I pulled up.

She steps forward slowly, sits on the arm of the sofa.

Do you want a divorce? he asks.

I don't know. Do you?

He's too tired to consider what he scarcely meant to ask.

Do you want to take a vacation? he says.

What about work?

Steering column needs fixing. And I saw a nor'easter coming up next week.

I don't want to take a vacation.

He nods, exhausted. He hasn't rested in going on thirty-six hours.

Can we talk about it over dinner?

He gestures to the coffee table, her name scrawled on another envelope.

She opens the note: *Good for one free bedroom door. Love, Leslie.*

OK, she says.

Les sleeps terribly.

He wakes with a shiver in his bones, an ache he fears might hollow him out. His eyes opening to a view of their bedroom, to the empty space beside Marlene, on their white sheets a glow from the snow-covered skylight. When he drifts back down, the image of the girl from the casino rises. She murmurs weakly into his ear.

★ ★ ★

MARLENE ROUSES IN the morning to the sound of Les bringing another bedroom door into their apartment. She hears him next in the kitchen, making coffee. She moves to the couch, where she wraps herself in the blanket he slept beneath last night, lays her head on the same pillow, the lingering scent of soap from his shower recalling the loss of Josie, not the arrival of Les.

They pass the day inside together with little said between them.

He throws on two coats of paint and drags the broken door out to the dumpster.

She reads the news, watches television, slips in and out of naps.

The windows cracked, the front door ajar, the day unseasonably warm and dry and bright.

At dinner they are seated at a back table as last time.

This . . . , he says of their day. This feels different.

Different how?

You don't agree?

I don't know.

My mitts and wits, he says, moving his fingers around freely. Marlene observes him withdraw into himself and return. Sometimes I see myself through you, he says. You're tough, rational. Those traits of yours become traits of mine on the boat. So many hours in my mind. Trying to look at myself from your perspective, or how I think you look at me, which usually isn't in the best light. Out there, I get trapped inside myself. This mean cycle that just replays. I can't put a price on what us getting along does to me. This. Here. Thinking you might still like me.

Marlene notices herself draw closer to her husband.

She sips her wine to avert her eyes.

Come on, let's get away for a little while, he says.

I can't.

Tell me why.

I just can't.

Let's go to Florida.

Absolutely not. I hate Florida.

It's not that bad.

It's where my parents live now and where you tried to ditch me.

It's a big state.

Your head is in the clouds, darling.

Marlene sees his face change. *Darling* escaped her mouth without consent, shot up from calloused depths, a dormant force of habit briefly awakened. She starts to say something and stops. She sips her wine again, half smiles. Around her the restaurant thrums. The chewing mouths, the glasses banging the bar top, the banter over a ball game on a wall-mounted set—she holds the simultaneity of the moment, bracing for what that word dredged up in her husband.

When you say *head in the clouds*, he says, do you mean like a blowjob in the sky?

Her burst of laughter draws attention from nearby tables.

You're stealing my bit, she says.

How am I doing?

It's a stretch.

Well, return the ball anyway, would you?

I said *your* head's in the clouds. Not I am going to *give you* head in the clouds.

Oh, alright, fair enough. He looks at his menu. What are we having?

I'm not sure yet. Let me see.

Her fingernails tap the table playfully.

A moment later he says, Could it be your subconscious?

Could what be my subconscious?

You know, somewhere buried inside maybe you got a hankering to give me blowjobs, ones that are so good they'll make me ecstatic like I floated up to the clouds?

Blow*jobs*, now?

Maybe?

You're pushing it.

But maybe?

The thought makes me nauseous.

Don't say that.

The sick rising up inside is a good indication that my subconscious and, for that matter, my plain uncomplicated conscious have zero desire to give you a blowjob, much less blow*jobs*.

Les nods, an overdone pout on his face.

Let's please change the subject, she says.

Good idea, he agrees. So, Florida?

She smiles again.

They sleep apart that night too. Marlene watches the lights from cars in the parking lot move across the wall, the same seconds replaying themselves for hours at a time. She considered letting Les into bed but in the end distrusted her instincts. She strains from the pull of separate and secret lives, racked up by the limbs and nearing the tear. In the other room Les says something from the depths of his dreams. She quiets, listens closely. There it is again, but it's not a word he utters. How long it's been since she's heard him laugh in his sleep.

WHEN LES WAKES in the morning, he feels lightened by the sudden presence in his life of an undashed blind hope. He believes Marlene will agree to a vacation. He also considers the need to talk to Alright about Hoover and Monk before leaving. A traitor, some will condemn him. A whore over family, over friends since little, will be their logic. Les speaks to John Wayne and China in his mind: A girl almost dying in his arms is reason to recalibrate his thinking this once.

He sees Marlene sitting up in bed.

She seems to not have slept at all.

He offers coffee.

She asks for tea.

On his way out the door, she has a second request, to which he agrees before she asks. He decides to not make his proposed getaway a bargaining chip. He will accumulate goodwill by exhibiting restraint. If she wants to borrow his truck for the day, that's fine by him.

He drives Marlene's car to Lutz's, sits outside the office, waits for Captain to arrive.

He casts a line off the dock.

He chats up the mechanics working on the boat, some flounder fisherman on a stopover.

He calls Alright's house before deciding to try the C-View.

When he arrives, Les is dismayed to see Booby there, too, kicking back Buds with the captain. In a booth near the back, Kathleen and Ethan huddle, the kid politely upright, pecking at a burger too big for his paws, his mom slurping down her Mount Gay and lime.

Les waves at his godson as he walks toward the bar.

Ethan waves back.

Les takes the stool next to Alright.

How long they been here? he asks.

Walked in an hour ago, Alright says.

Stumbled in, Booby corrects him.

Jesus Christ, JW, Les says.

Kathleen and Les make eye contact.

He smiles. She rolls her eyes.

What's going on, Stray? the bartender asks.

Les says he isn't thirsty.

Listen, he says to Alright, I may be cutting out of town for a little while. You let me know when we're going out again?

Gonna be after the nor'easter.

I'm countin' on it.

Alright, he says.

Les looks over at Booby. He questions whether or not to speak up in front of him. But he's already worked out the details and settled on his decision. Booby being here might mitigate the betrayal some—at least Les will say it to his face.

There's another thing.

Alright sets his beer down.

Well, let's have it, Stray.

Les proceeds to tell Captain about Hoover and Monk's habit, what he himself has seen, his suspicion of drugs on board, the wildness of the other night at the casino, the two girls and the one that almost died. He tries to keep it short, feeling from the start the agitation held back behind Alright's flat expression. But it's Booby's indifference, not once interrupting, not once countering, that troubles Les. As if he's already primed Alright for this possibility.

It's not how things are done, I get it, Les finishes. But we tried going to Booby first.

Any of this why you attacked Hoover? Alright asks.

Les shakes his head.

What'd you do that for?

Les doesn't answer.

Alright and Booby share a look.

I told you he's got something against my nephew. They all do. Brutal what Stray did, and he won't explain it. Or is it me you got a problem with, boy? You think you'd be a better mate?

Of course I would.

You see, Captain? Just like I said.

I don't want your job, Booby.

Cut it out, Alright says. You've known Hoover since he was young, Stray. And Booby helped bring you up. This the course you want to chart after you kicked his ass? Don't get me wrong, I don't want drugs on my boat—and Lord knows there's always problems with the crew—but what the hell is happening to you all? JW slapped Monk, is that right? China's working extra hard to lose this job, from what I'm told. And you cursed your old man? I know you're dealing with a lot at home. Is that it, son? You got to have a reason for attacking Hoover. Help me understand.

Les lowers his voice: Hoover pissed on JW's kid at the party.

Pissed on Ethan? Booby says. My ass.

Keep your voice down, Les snaps.

There's anger in you, son, Alright says.

He pissed on his hands and then rubbed them all over the kid's head.

That's crazy. We were all there. Nobody pissed on anybody.

You weren't outside when he leaked on his hands.

No, but I was inside when you broke his face.

You sure he didn't accidentally drip on his hands?

Yes, I'm fucking sure.

Calm, Alright warns.

I'm sure.

'Cause dripping will happen.

What are you saying, Captain?

I'm just saying it happens sometimes.

It wasn't an accident.

It happens to me more than I'd like to admit.

I'm not making this up, dammit.

I know, I know.

He rubbed piss on the boy without anybody noticing.

Bullshit, Booby says.

Well, true or not, it's good you kept it quiet alright. JW would go Hulk on Hoover.

Kathleen's sudden presence at the bar curbs their conversation. She turns to Les as the bartender gives back her change.

I didn't choose this sorry place, she says, nodding to Ethan. *He* wanted to come here.

She walks back to the booth, picks up her son.

They watch her carry him to the entrance.

Her middle finger raised high as she opens the door with her hip.

You're not very good at making friends, are you, Stray? Alright says.

A girl almost died, Les says, zipping up his jacket. You two keep forgetting that.

He follows Kathleen and Ethan to the parking lot, watches her open the passenger door and Ethan climb in. They drive off. Les trails close behind. To his relief she stays in her lane, maintains the speed limit, signals when appropriate. At a stoplight, she and Ethan jump out of the car, the boy from shotgun and Kathleen from the driver's seat, and together they race clockwise around the vehicle, laughing hysterically in the cold and screaming at the top of their lungs about some fire in China and the bees in their bonnets. He follows onward, all the way to John Wayne's new house. She escorts the kid to the front door, kneeling to give him a long hug and kiss—a goodbye, Les realizes, after Ethan goes inside and John Wayne comes out and she throws her arms around him too. They hold each other, swaying beneath the covered porch, protected from the snow just now falling. Then she turns and walks away. Les feels ashamed for watching.

MARLENE DRAGS HER cigarette, gazes through the windshield as she passes The Villas, squaring the blocks around the motel. She didn't sleep last night. Torn between lives, she has no way to keep herself whole. In bed, then, she grieved the arrival of day, unsure how to act when the sun came up or who to be. She mourned the night, too, letting it into her sheets as though she were losing another mother. As light began to color the room, worry gnawed at her, and she decided to visit The Villas again, to witness in day what she's only ever seen at dark, and to maybe catch a fleeting glimpse of Josie. But this time from the elevated cab of Les's anonymous truck.

At an intersection, window cracked, she hears the crash of the ocean in the distance. How has she not noticed the sound before? This little township, once intertwined with the commerce of the sea, has always felt so far from shore. Beyond the time-keeping of the waves she hears the low hum of power lines, the crackling of tobacco leaves, a plastic bottle whipping across the sidewalk, the flick of a streetlight changing. Absent are the blows and clicks of a train running down the sinking tracks, the hiss and pop of a truck's exhaust break, the grinding gears and high candle flame of a factory, long closed, from which smoke once pooled into the sky like a faucet underwater.

The story of this town seems to replay every generation, word passing from person to person, moving through community centers, churches, parks, and counsel meetings, articulated in editorials and featured on the nightly news—the collapse of industry and the desperation of locals. From this place hope diverged, fled in all four directions: From the boom of their whaling ancestors, four or five generations ago, the rough-worn men wrangling the great beasts in the bay waters and the ingenious women inventing endless ways to repurpose the bone and blubber left devastated by the species' migration north; to the lumberjacks and shipbuilders about which Marlene's grandmother proudly boasted—skilled, brave men who lost life and limb to the thousand-year-old widow-makers they felled until the pinelands stood barren and labor moved south to Destiny and beyond, where railroads converged and the shipping channels were dug and the metallic monoliths Les fished on today arrived from steel towns to the west; to the fish factories a few decades ago, sheet metal hangars with their gravel parking lots abandoned but for the lingering smell of rotting bi-catch and innards, where men and women alike, many exiting taverns at sunup or roused still drunk in phone booths, grabbed burlap bags off a stack of pallets and began shucking the daily catch for a unit price, the dignity of work making for easy camaraderie until these same cutting motions became the jobs of fisherman no longer working day trips but out for longer and longer spells at sea, farther and farther east into the unknown; to, finally, the promise of tourism and real estate resurgence for single-story second homes, disappointment fleeing in no direction this time because the successful working class and small businesses never arrived and so hope could not depart. And now the views from the shore just an earshot from Marlene are reduced to the slow crawl of commercial trawlers, fishholds full, from all across the Eastern Seaboard, and of million-dollar blow boats swept in from locales that can afford the technologies of leisure and nostalgia.

Her hand begins to shake.

The grim condition of this town calls Bill to mind, his perch on top of this forsaken place. How had she not helped more, not gathered here mornings, alone or with two or three others, to pick trash or serve hot tea, provide fresh food and toiletries, tents to those sleeping under cardboard beneath the underpasses? With their sturdy backs and bounties from sweet meat shipped off to Manhattan, London, Tokyo, the whole fishing crew could've parked on shoulders and side streets, bracing against the wind, and tried, just tried, to see beyond themselves into the lives of others.

Her forearm seizes next.

As she swings around the block The Villas returns to view. Josie is still nowhere to be seen. There are a few girls in the enclosure, waiting out their sputtering highs. The motel lies desolate, the cold pressing into the walls. The towering sign flickers before the gray, pregnant sky, the snow beginning to fall, flakes light as ash.

Now there's a twitch in her biceps.

She turns desperately toward home.

This is what madness looks like.

The body shakes until parts of the mind start to detach.

The nearer she gets to her apartment, the calmer she feels, and once she parks, Marlene is thankful to have arrived before Les. She climbs the exterior stairwell, wanting a moment to settle her nerves. In front of her door, a body shivers, hospital gown damp, toes turning blue. As she rushes to Josie, lifting her up, Marlene notices the tremor in her arm has stopped.

LES PARKS NEXT to his truck, the step down from her car short compared to the drop he's used to. He peers into his cab, sees suitcases packed and loaded. He didn't question why Marlene wanted to borrow his truck this morning. Now he understands that she wanted to surprise him. They are going away together.

He takes the stairs two at a time, calls her name as he flings open the door. She peers up from her seat at the kitchen table, steam rising from two mugs. Next to her is a woman in his wife's clothes. Les halts with recognition.

Marlene watches them share a look.

I need your help, she says.

The jump in her lilt draws Les from the girl back to his wife.

He closes and locks the door, walks over, stands behind a chair.

What's going on?

I can't go into everything right now.

Can you give me something?

We don't have a lot of time.

He nods, not knowing what to say, still stunned by the girl's presence.

Marlene takes a moment to collect her thoughts.

I've been . . .

She shakes off a smile, glances at Josie, then back to her mug.

For the past several . . . , Marlene tries a second time.

She holds back a laugh again.

Well, sit down, would you? she snaps at Les. You're making me nervous.

Les sits down.

Nights you're gone, I bring home . . .

Marlene cannot contain the laughter bursting from her this time.

It's delirious and childlike.

She calms herself, juts her chin out proudly.

She turns to Josie in order to get out her words to Les.

I've been bringing home prostitutes from The Villas for months whenever you're gone. We spend time with each other, that's all. Make dinner, stuff like that. I know how it sounds to you. I can hear your tiny thoughts. And I don't care. You don't need to say anything. Please don't, actually. Just keep your mouth shut.

Les isn't sure whether the disdain in her tone is for him or because she is ashamed of admitting all of this aloud. In any case, he sits there at once disturbed by her secrets and relieved to finally know something truthful about her. He heard the parallel story as well, the one Marlene purposefully omits: the failed therapy, the grief group meditations, the slow isolation and distancing, the bullshit fight with her parents, the great psychological burden of a double life. He jams his thumb into his stomach, but the bruise has dulled, its throb unreachable.

Why? he asks.

Because I have no one. Because I'm alone.

The reality of her words breaks over Marlene's face.

Les is thankful she's looked away.

We can help her, Marlene says. We've got to get her out of town.

He's uncomfortable, too, because it's been years since he's felt needed by her.

This is all it takes to get you to go away with me? he jokes.

You son of a bitch, Marlene says. How's it so easy for you? How has it always been so easy? You've been running away from me since the day we met. You stayed gone, gone, gone. And then you joke about where I end up? So far away from myself, so far from where I hoped to be. You think that's funny? She looks him dead in the eye. Choose me. Choose me this once. Choose your wife. You're never going to get another chance. We've needed to go back for a while. This is why. I'm certain of it. I see it now. All of it finally makes some sense. We can be a family. You and me and Josie. The three of us down in Destiny.

His thoughts twist up at the certainty of her delusion.

He remembers the Marlene of another season: She walks him across the field, their shadows long and dark over the knee-high rye. Her face freckled by summer, hair caught in her mouth as she glances at him and smiles, soft eyes falling on him like a whisper.

Yes, OK. Yes.

Say it. Say, I choose you. I choose my wife.

Yes, OK. I choose you, Marlene. I choose my wife.

TWELVE

The land turns porous as they drive the eight hours to Destiny. The coastline, at first a yellow pelt laid down along the shore, slowly disintegrates in the rising tide. Hour after hour the grasses retreat from the encroaching water. The ocean creeps in for miles, pushing all the way up to the interstate, all the way to the backs of houses, where dry docks become wet docks, hoisted boats suddenly afloat, windswept meadows temporarily drowned, swaying exaltedly beneath the sea. The entire trip Josie also oscillates, between sobs and sleep. With her eyes closed, Les and Marlene keep the radio down, small talk to a minimum, whispering to each other whenever they feel confident that she rests easy. When awake, she stares out the window, forehead to glass. Sometimes she stirs and says she made a mistake. She wants to go back.

He needs me, she says. We need each other.

Marlene tells Les to keep driving.

She climbs into the backseat, lets Josie doze on her lap, works a hand through her hair.

They drive like this, Les in front and Marlene and Josie in back, until the mile marker reads zero and the speed limit plummets and a lane drops away just before a bridge that stretches over a wide dredged canal. A mile and a half down a county highway, the tree line falls back off the road and the thirty acres where Marlene grew up opens before them.

Windows down, the air is sharp.

Crocuses blossom near the pond, daffodils, too, pushing up color from the thawing soil, their purples, yellows, and greens the earliest exertions of spring. The field, typically leased to hay farmers, has been tilled for large-scale production, plowed in long, wandering lines, the furrows dusted with snow. Geese preen on the property's far bend. The two-story colonial now visible through a wall of evergreens.

Marlene looks at Les pleadingly through the rearview.

No, he says.

Yes, she says.

He's clearly leased to some serious folk this year.

They'll never know it was us.

You are such a spoiled brat.

He swerves the truck off the road and they tear through the field, Marlene turning giddy, Josie bolting upright. Les figure-eights, kicks up mud, and bounces over plow lines. The wind flushes their cheeks, combs through their hair. Les straightens out the wheel as he pulls up behind the geese. The flock lifts together and streaks low across the earth. The truck gives chase, Les pounding the horn amid their honks, the birds so near the windows that the three of them can almost reach out and touch one. The geese shift direction in unison. They open their wings and rise, drift back to a corner of the field. Les slows to a crawl again when the truck crosses over into the lawn and he glimpses Marlene's bright eyes begin to dim. He takes the rear way up to the house, rolling through the grass in the backyard, purposefully avoiding the driveway.

AT THE TABLE that night Marlene and Les wait, dinner laid out over a yellowed lace tablecloth. Candlelight smolders in the sterling cutlery. It quivers overhead in the near ceiling. Les had opened the house when they first arrived, removing the sheets from furniture, unsealing the windows to air out the place, as Marlene made dinner, pulling what she could find from the deep freeze. No one had been here for quite a while, and they were both relieved that the gas and electric functioned fine. Even the landline still worked.

Josie refused to leave the guest room, except for one time. She'd lost her cell at the hospital and slipped downstairs to try Bill on the house phone. Marlene wasn't fooled. She ended the call as Josie started to dial. Marlene then locked the receiver in the desk beside the back door and hid the key under the sink.

Marlene pushes her chair back and stands.

They hear floorboards creak at the top of the stairs.

Josie sulks down, enters the dining room, and takes her place.

Marlene serves Josie and herself before passing the food to Les.

Eat, Marlene says. And don't say you're not hungry. That I won't believe.

I'm not hungry.

You couldn't tell, Marlene says to Les, but this one eats me out of house and home.

Marlene sits.

Josie takes a bite, puts down her spoon.

Stew too gamey? Marlene asks. The venison won't be much better, but you should try some.

She doesn't wait for an answer. She's back on her feet, serving up a coin of backstrap, cutting it into small squares, coating each piece in a touch of grease.

Les and Josie share a smile, eyes bulging at her meticulousness.

Marlene notices.

I'm telling you, Les. I've never met a little thing with such a big appetite.

I believe you.

She puts the venison down in front of Josie and sits again.

Josie takes another bite, chews, opens her mouth to show Les.

He laughs, looking away.

Before long, Josie's just moving the food around on her plate.

Maybe skip to desert? Marlene says. She begins to get up again.

I saw some ice—

I don't want ice cream.

What do you want?

Josie gives Marlene an impatient look.

You can't have a phone. You can have anything but that.

Heroin? she jokes, glancing at Les.

Les doesn't laugh. He also doesn't shy from eye contact.

How about booze? he says.

Marlene hears a note of familiarity in their exchange.

She nods at Les to make Josie a drink.

He goes to the kitchen, returns with a finger of rum.

Josie chugs the drink as soon as he sets it down.

This used to be the kitchen, Marlene says, filling up the silence. That was the dining room.

Josie follows Marlene's eyes to the room behind her. She turns to look: a crimson-and-black area rug beneath a high arch-legged table; a gold damask love seat with matching armchairs; a glass case housing dusty books, pottery, figurines; an antique secretary desk on the back wall.

What's that room now?

A sitting room.

A sitting room? Josie repeats, boredom nearing mockery.

Yes, a sitting room.

What do you do in a sitting room?

Well, sit, I guess. Take tea.

Take tea?

Yes, take tea, Marlene says defensively. No one ever uses it.

You have rooms in your house nobody uses?

It's not my house, but, yes, my parents put an extension on about ten years ago.

Right. An extension.

Why do you keep repeating everything I say? They bought this house fifty years ago when it was condemned. They planted almost every living thing on the property: the orchard, the flower beds, the trees. They brought this place back to life, turned into a working gentleman's farm.

An orchard?

Marlene glares at Les, recalling his spoiled-brat remark from earlier.

And a gentleman's farm?

You showed up at my door, remember?

Can I have another drink? Josie asks.

Yes, please, Marlene says.

Les doesn't bother with glasses this time. He brings the bottle back instead.

Josie downs her drink in a gulp again.

Marlene wants to slap her.

My folks couldn't afford to buy this house, even at auction. My dad was a landscaper back then. My mom's parents gave him a loan. And then my folks rebuilt this place one detail at a time, one room at a time, over decades. They put their life into it. It was a ghost land before them.

It still feels like a ghost land, Josie says.

Don't be cruel, Les says.

Seriously, where is everyone? Why does no one live here anymore?

I'm asking nice, he says. Turn it down a notch.

Well, you say something, then.

About what?

About this weird family dinner.

Show a little respect.

Wow, OK, Josie says. So you're Dad now. She looks at them, then at the room. Bill was right. Your colors are spoiled. Now you get the Destiny you always wanted: house, family, kids.

Kid, Marlene says.

What?

Kid. One. Kid.

Kid. One. Kid, Josie repeats. Lucky me.

She shoves back her chair and stands.

Sit your ass down, Marlene says.

Josie glares at her as she takes her seat.

All that money I saved on my own for years, Marlene says. For the house I was going to build. Thirty-five thousand dollars. Nearly none of it left. Bill has it all, doesn't he? Because if you had any of it yourself, you'd have options. There'd be other places for you to go. I guess that makes us both pretty stupid.

May I be excused? Josie asks.

She picks up her plate to take into the kitchen.

Just leave it, Marlene says.

Josie grabs the bottle of rum instead, the plate rattling on the table as she flees upstairs.

Marlene takes another bite, not avoiding eye contact with Les. She sees the full hilarity of the situation, the irony with which Les and Josie must judge her: Grief-stricken Marlene forcing a mother-daughter dynamic on woman paid to fulfill fantasies. But she won't be dismissed so simply. Something important just happened at this table. They all sensed it. She feels it prickling at the edges of her skin. The whole dinner felt like a bizarre near parody only genuine families ever approximate. Not despite the conflict, but because of it. She tries to come up with some joke to clue Les in to her way of thinking. Next, she searches herself for anger, some resentment she can marshal in his direction. But that, too, refuses to rise.

THEY DO THE dishes together, open some wine, drape coats over their shoulders, and step out to the backyard. Les lights two Merits, hands one to Marlene. Then he gets to work on the chiminea while Marlene loads a bowl. They pass a pipe back and forth, relax into their chairs, and watch the wet woodsmoke until the fire rolls and flames leap up out of the stack.

Marlene breaks the quiet.

The guy she's running from—I think he's violent with them.

Les listens as she recounts the story, understanding it's meant to persuade him of something of which he needs no convincing. He doesn't want to hear about Bill right now. The scars under Josie's arm, which he will continue to keep from Marlene, remain vivid in his mind. He doesn't need this evening explained either. He's embarrassed for her, embarrassed himself for getting swept up in the strangeness, embarrassed for the obedience Josie showed Marlene after she yelled. He spent the car ride down watching them in the rearview. He wondered where the money came from, surmised her house savings, but even if not, even if it was from his scalloping, he cared less about the numbers than the cost of how far afield Marlene's dreams had been dragged and dumped. He couldn't judge her. He couldn't be angry with her. Everything she hasn't given up freely has been ripped from her. Besides, he can't remember the last time she wasn't furious with him. It's just the opposite. She wants him to understand. She wants him to see.

You and Josie know each other from somewhere, she says.

No, why?

You recognized her at our apartment.

I was just caught off guard, that's all.

Les tosses some more kindling into the fire.

What about tonight? Marlene persists. You two seemed natural with each other.

Probably because you were there.

He sits back down.

You'll help protect her, right?

I will, sure, he says. What's the plan?

What do you mean?

How are we going to help her?

The three of us. Down here in Destiny.

Right, but then what?

That's the plan.

You mean for good? You're joking.

There's silence between them.

I told you this already.

Behind the tree line, the lights of the town make a hologram out of a low drift of clouds. But just above the house, the night darker, there is a cold, milky twilight, and Les, changing the subject, points to the gleaming sky. Marlene holds out her hand and Les takes it without breaking from the theater overhead. They spend the night like this, sparking one cigarette off the last, their eyes licked with flames.

Looks like we'll have to deal with a hormonal teenager after all, she says.

Les pretends he doesn't hear.

★ ★ ★

THE NEXT MORNING Marlene awakens in the most exquisitely familiar way. The wind whistles outdoors. The bones of the house stretch. The shadow of a tree trembles in a square of light on the floorboards. She doesn't shudder when she realizes that her head rests on Les's chest. She nestles closer, pulls the blanket to her chin. Her nose cold but her body warm. Last night the weed heightened the awkwardness as they stripped for bed and did not have sex. There is the possibility that it will happen now as they fall in and out of shallow sleep, Les rubbing the small of her back. But they hear Josie across the hall and Marlene gets up to check on her.

She shares the guest bed with Josie for most of the day.

They remain in pajamas, eat lunch up there, play cards, read the newspaper.

Their dynamic remains injured.

You can't be mad at me forever, Marlene says in the early afternoon.

An army of bullfrogs, Josie replies, turning an article to show her. They call them armies, if you can believe it. Marlene tries to interject, but Josie begins to read out loud. *As winter passes, the American bullfrog has been notoriously absent from the southeastern United States. Early signs point to the likelihood that a great migration to a new hibernating locale occurred, nearly undetected, this past fall. Several residents just outside of Destiny recently claimed to have sighted the amphi . . .* Josie stops there, summarizes instead. The paper says some people around here think they've spotted the bullfrogs, but nothing verified yet. Wild, right, them waking up this far north?

Did you hear what I said?

Josie reads more of the article aloud.

American bullfrogs are unlikely to cross the canal as the water is salty and too highly trafficked. She looks up from the paper. Guess how people discovered they weren't down there? In the South. The males form choruses, breeding choruses. It sounds likes bulls. You can't miss it. The sound is so intense you can feel it on your skin. The noise hasn't shown up this spring. The land thawed or whatever, everybody just waiting, and there was . . . nothing.

I want you to think of this place as your home.

Listen to yourself.

There's nothing keeping you from living here.

You're crazy.

Just consider it.

You know I used to think I was from a darker world than you. But I get to leave these fantasies. I get to dip in and out of them, you know?

There's so much space and it's just going to waste.

But you're stuck inside this fantasy for good, aren't you?

I'm offering you another way to live.

You're offering me another role to play.

Just think about it. You'll think about it, won't you?

I'll stay for a little. But I'm not staying for good.

Marlene goes to the door, stopping at the edge.

American bullfrogs in Destiny, huh?

An army of them.

That sound like bulls.

In breeding choruses.

Imagine that?

This goes on for several days. Josie upstairs, refusing to leave the room. Marlene with her for much of the time, walking away from these conversations feeling like she's closer to persuading Josie to stay. When not in the house, Marlene runs errands. Trash and recycling drop-off, drugstore, hardware. At the supermarket she conquers the cereal aisle with ease. Her life feels focused, each step imbued with meaning, actions decisively linked to the last, to the next. On the drive home one day she improvises, cruises alongside a stretch of beach. The rolling fog dissolves town. Left are the faintly drawn slack of power lines, the washed-out flags posted to electrical poles, slatted sand fences lining a gloomy path to the sea. She stops at the lighthouse. The lantern room plunges up into the haze. Marlene sits on the hood, takes in the air with deep, thankful swallows.

LES DEVOTES HIS days to working on Marlene's father's boat out in the barn. He aims to take them on a run to sea before the nor'easter and he tells Marlene as much to justify his time away from the house, time away from her. The first few nights, he enjoyed sitting outside with his wife, narrating stories of how the stars animate so vividly over the remote waters of the planet. But the old roads of their conversations are beat to gravel. Not only does she refuse to recognize the absurdity of her plan, growing frustrated with his subtle prodding, but in the hours they spend together he realizes that Josie is the lone subject that feels firm beneath their feet. Behind their silence, hidden in all their quiet, he hears the whisper of his daughter's name and he finds himself pulled back relentlessly to the escape of scalloping.

Any progress up there? he asks on the third night.

Why do you say it like that?

He hears the impatience steeped in his voice, a restlessness they both recognize.

He suppresses the urge to add another log to the chiminea.

I didn't say it any way.

I want you to finally quit fishing, she says.

What made you think that right now?

I know how your mind works.

It's a bad time. The crew is a mess.

When's it ever a good time?

I'll think about it, he says.

OK. Good.

Les gestures up to the light in the guest room.

Yes, progress. I think so, she says.

What's that look like?

I think she'll come downstairs soon.

Does she have family?

There's that tone of voice again.

Parents? Friends?

Her life's a mess.

Staying for a little makes sense.

Staying for longer makes more.

You got to see this for what it is.

Why are you picking a fight? We're having a nice time and you're picking a fight.

I'm not trying to fight.

Good, then let's talk about something other than Josie.

I want to help.

Literally anything else, please!

The next day Josie comes downstairs for the first time since storming out of the dining room. Les is in the barn, beneath the hull of the boat, a brush in his hand and a smoke in his teeth. Marlene's gone for a drive.

Hey, Josie says.

He looks up.

She holds two beers.

You come to help? I could use it.

I heard the radio.

I'm doing the bottom with ablative paint just now. It wears off over the course of a few years. Kind of like a bar of soap. Grab a brush. A mask too.

You're not wearing one.

He rubs out his cigarette on the concrete.

I should be.

They work together on their backs, painting under the boat, bow to stern.

You going to tell her how we know each other? Josie asks.

Not sure how to begin that conversation.

What do you mean?

See, honey—Les says, pretending to address Marlene—my buddies and me were at a casino with a couple of hookers . . .

Those idiots are your buddies?

This Bill guy's a stand-up dude from what I've heard.

You saved my life.

I lied to her.

They go back to painting the hull.

What are those scars above your ribs? he says.

You saw those? What else did you see? she jokes.

He puts down his brush.

Two of them looked pretty fresh.

Yeah.

Bill?

She nods.

Your daughter died down here, didn't she? Josie says. It's why the house is abandoned.

A sudden swell stops just behind Les eyes. It settles in his jaw, the taste metallic.

I'm not her stand-in, she says.

I know.

But does Marlene?

I'm sorry she yelled at you the other night at the table.

Josie's face flushes.

What? he asks.

I'm not used to apologies, I guess.

They hear the truck honk in the backyard.

Why won't she use the driveway?

Come on, he says.

They follow the bluestone footpath around the house, pass beneath the sprawling magnolia, find Marlene staging shopping bags on the back porch. She startles to see the two of them emerge from around the house. You're out of your room, she says.

No, I'm out of *your* room, Josie replies.

In the kitchen, Les and Josie unpack the bags. Marlene puts the groceries away.

You two working on the boat?

Josie's helping me with the ablative.

You wearing gloves?

Yes, we are wearing gloves.

And masks?

And masks.

Wait . . . Oh, man, I almost forgot. Josie says, grabbing the local newspaper. On the countertop, she opens to a color image of a frog sitting on a patch of lawn. They've been spotted here, she says. American bullfrogs. It's official. It's real.

They crossed the canal?

A few of them, I guess.

A hobby of ours, Marlene says to Les.

I knew I'd seen one before, Josie goes on, tapping the photo. With my parents down in Georgia visiting my dad's folks. I was way young then but I remember going to this alligator farm, if you can imagine. A trip to an alligator farm? Apparently, the gators can only see in black and white, so they feed them marshmallows to get them to do tricks. Stupid tricks, too, like climb up on a log or come on out of the water. Like, who cares? Still, what a life those gators lived! I mean, hanging in a warm bath, eating marshmallows all day? That was fun and good and a little scary for obvious reasons, but what really stole the show that day was when we stumbled on an American bullfrog the size of a football and in its mouth was a dang mouse with its nose and little beady eyes poking out. What's funny is how calm the mouse was, like it was home and protected. Then its claws started scampering and guess what? Gulp. That little mouse went right down the throat and the frog just sat there staring at us like there wasn't a thing out of the ordinary, can you believe it? Then it let out this huge ribbit, like a belch. I remember someone saying then that these bullfrogs eat everything. Like everything. I mean. Every. Thing.

Her rush of words clutters the silence that succeeds them.

Aren't you just a diesel-powered icebreaker? Les says.

I guess somebody's feeling better, Marlene adds.

Where are your parents now? he asks.

My mom's in Phoenix. She's sober. She writes sometimes. Dad I don't know.

Marlene glares at Les.

I should finish the ablative before dark, he says.

I'll come too.

Wait, no, stay, Marlene says. Tell me more about the bullfrogs.

Josie halts, the corners of her mouth dropping.

It's fine, Marlene says. You can go.

No, no. I'll stay.

You can go.

No, really, it's fine, I'll stay, Josie says as she slips out the door, chasing after Les.

DAY BY DAY Josie spends more time out in the barn. They change the oil, replace the spark plugs and zinc before affixing the outboard to the stern; they inflate the trailer's tires, lubricate the bearings; they wax and buff the fiberglass, hull and topside. Marlene gets the progress reports at lunch and dinner. She doesn't like being alone indoors for spells of hours, the wind carrying the sounds of the radio and laughter up to the house. But she can also hardly conceive of a walk out to the barn. She considers taking the roundabout path along the tree line, coming up on them broadside, but then she'll have to explain why she refuses to return to the house across the driveway. So Marlene keeps away, mulching in the backyard or reading indoors, news of the nor'easter making landfall tomorrow. Besides, Josie is acclimating despite her wish to leave, and Les's thoughts are off scalloping. She's also intrigued by their dynamic, the connection she's observed still mystifying her.

At one point she hears Josie scream and she tears out onto the front porch, heart cut through with terror. Josie is fine—elated, in fact. Les has backed the boat up to the spigot off the side of the house, screwed the hose into the water intake of the outboard, thrown the gear into neutral, and pulled the starter. Josie jumps with joy at the roll of the engine and the stream of water shooting from the pump, the boat all prepped for the season.

Now or never, he says.

Now, now, now, Josie says.

Les looks to Marlene. How about you, Mama?

Sure, she says. I'll grab my coat. Pick me up around back.

They run east to start, into the endless expanse of sea, the land behind them fading to shadows. They run straight at the sun shining down on the water like a bright broadening path, straight into a sea made of light. Les sits at the helm with Josie, Marlene reclining on a bench on the other side of the console. In the chill of the wind and heat of the sun they pass around a blanket Marlene finds in a storage compartment. At one point they come into a swell and a small pod of dolphins swim alongside them. Les shows Josie how to work the throttle to ride the waves, the dolphins following her as she surfs the chop. They drink lukewarm beer, eat pretzels for lunch, idling for a time, their faces like reptiles' turned to the sun. After, Les heads back to land. The coast rises up out of the sea again, and Josie, disoriented, thinks they've come upon some far-off island.

They return to Destiny through the inlet, motor past marinas, the boardwalk, waterside restaurants, elevator cranes, drawbridge, lumber mills, and processing plants. As they cross the length of the canal, Marlene points out where her family's land backs up to the water. She works in concert with Les, reading his every need on the boat, knowing, for example, when to take the helm as he throws a net for bunker fish along the rocks. Scoring dozens and storing them in the bait well, they run out to the rips, spend an hour trolling for bluefish without success. Les switches controls to the tower, invites Josie up top with him, hands her his polar-ized sunglasses.

Marlene observes from her bench below them.

Look for birds, she hears him say.

Josie points to a stretch of sea where several dozen gannets flitter and dive.

What do you see? he asks.

Looks like it's raining on the water.

She glances, confused, up at the clear sky.

We found our bluefish, he says. They're in a feeding frenzy. Take us over there slow.

Marlene is already reeling in the trolling rods. She loads the hooks with their biggest bunker, weights the lines with lead, hands one to Josie once she climbs back down to deck. They drop lines into the water just as Les turns the boat into the bait ball. Beneath them, tens of thousands of fish churn the water into a boil and they wait for a rod to dip. But the sea goes calm again as quickly as it erupted. Not a single tug on their lines.

Les can only laugh in disbelief as the roiling water migrates away.

Marlene laughs, too, saying, Not our day.

I'm not giving up yet.

Last trick up his sleeve is a bayside run on the way back to the truck. They tear down the coastline before turning into a small man-made channel, enormous houses with private docks standing one after the other on either side. By the time they reach the end of the water cul-de-sac, Marlene has removed the sinkers and added floaters. Les flips the throttle to neutral and Marlene hands him the rod as she takes the helm.

Your dad's lucky lure, he says to Marlene.

Don't hook it on the dock.

Les casts the line about fifteen yards, the lure landing just to the side of a piling.

He adjusts the drag before handing the rod to Josie.

Stripers are enormous down here. They like the—

Josie yells.

The line is already running.

Raise the tip, Les says, helping her. That's it—higher.

She raises the rod tip.

Good, good. Reel, reel, reel, reel.

The fish is too powerful; Josie can't crank the handle.

Reel, reel, reel, Les repeats, excited.

She struggles. The reel won't budge. The line is still running.

Josie tries to hand the rod to Les.

You do it, you do it, he says. Come on.

She uses all her strength and the handle snaps cleanly off, the line continuing to run.

Her mood drops as she looks to Les with the broken parts in her hand.

Let it run, let it run, he says.

Marlene watches him take the rod from Josie without registering her expression.

He's already removing the broken handle and affixing a new one to the reel.

I'm sorry, Josie says. I lost the lucky lure.

It's OK, Marlene says. Don't worry about it.

You hooked him great, Les says. Are you kidding me? Now we got to find him.

Just cut the line, Marlene says. Let's go home.

We're not losing this fish.

The reel ripping off line stops. The striper finally comes to a halt.

It could be anywhere, Marlene complains.

I know. That's the fun.

Les holds out the fixed rod to Josie.

At the bow, she reels slowly.

The line pulls taut as she cranks, aiming them to the piling where the lure first landed.

Marlene returns to the helm, motors them closer.

No way it's still under there, she says. It's zigzagged every one of these docks, I bet.

She steers them right up to the piling, and Les, leaning halfway off the boat, asks for the rod. Josie hands it to him. He reaches out as far as he can, just short of falling overboard, and threads the rod around the piling, loosening up more line.

Josie helps him back on board, then she reels in the slack again.

The line leads them to another dock, all the way across the waterway.

See? Marlene says, motoring them to the next spot.

Here, Les climbs onto a private dock, lies flat on his stomach, hanging over the edge to feed the rod between pilings. The owner comes out, two terriers yapping alongside. Marlene and Josie laugh as Les rolls off and splashes into the water.

He swims back, shivering.

They find the striper at the fifth dock beneath a hoisted boat.

Lips blue from cold, Les slides on waders and boots and drops into the shallow water again.

He trudges over.

The striper emerges from the murk, approaches him with each half turn of the reel.

He pulls the fish into view and leads it up to the boat.

Josie's grin is winsome and pure.

Marlene's too.

She hands him the disgorger and he removes the hook from the striper's mouth.

Josie hangs over the side and Les shows her how to grip the bottom lip to keep hold.

Like sandpaper, she says.

Marlene stretches her mouth into a smile on seeing Les appreciate this small success of parenthood and Josie grateful to be shown a gesture of care, of reliance. She waits for a rush of delight to fill her up. But none comes and she's left bewildered by the emptiness. When Les and Josie then turn to share the joy of the moment, she feels exposed in the mirror of their eyes, staggering from seeing herself as they must see her: a proud and desperate mother, false smile twisted by grief, a little bent, a little broken.

The fish closes its mouth on Josie's finger and she yelps.

The striper swims away.

OUTSIDE, THE WIND roars wildly, circling the house as if from every direction. Hail slows to snow, then quickens to rain spattering the rooftop and windows. The nor'easter has not let up since morning. The three of them spent the day indoors, rigging up rabbit ears to watch the weather report. Now, in the living room, Les keeps an eye on Marlene, who's been staring at the same magazine page for hours. She's felt far away since the end of yesterday's boat ride, fully and finally gone after last night. They still haven't spoken about what happened in bed.

Les made a move, running a finger along her thigh.

Marlene shivered from his cold hand and pulled him on top.

Les watched her eyes open to him, turn away, open to him, and wince.

He wasn't sure if he was being scrutinized. Or if she was afraid of him scrutinizing her.

He flicked off the lamp.

Her breath coming in short shots until he gathered it was a word she kept repeating.

Stop, she demanded in the dark. Stop.

She rolled over, wrenching him painfully from inside of her.

All day she refused to explain her reaction; he'd not gathered the courage to ask.

In the late afternoon Josie announced that she'd cook dinner. She spends hours in the kitchen, Les and Marlene restricted from entering, from even setting the table. They sit in the living room, hands busy with cigarettes, pretending not to ignore each other. The fireplace rolls. The radio dialed to the only station with a signal: steel drum covers of reggae hits. Lightning hews the trees out of the night.

Dinner is served, Josie calls from the kitchen.

This ought to be interesting, Marlene says.

The dining table looks as it has the past several nights except Marlene moves the glasses and utensils to the proper side of the plates. She takes her time deliberately, Les notices, and Josie observes these corrections as she brings in a casserole dish.

Wala, Josie says.

Voilà, Marlene corrects her.

Josie removes the lid to reveal a bubbling top of melted cheese.

What do you think? she says.

What is it? Marlene asks.

You've never had it before?

Had *what*, dear?

Mexican lasagna.

One more time, please?

Mexican lasagna.

Wala indeed.

Les eats a helping and goes back for seconds when he sees Marlene picking at the edge of her plate. She sets her fork down and Les is surprised by how willing she is to approach indignation. He figured her fight was with him. Now he's not so sure.

You don't like it? Josie asks.

I do, Marlene says. It's just . . .

Just what?

I don't like nachos.

But it's not nachos.

Right, I know. After a pause, she asks, What exactly is in it?

Tortilla chips, beans, ground beef, cheese, salsa, sour cream.

I see. So, how's it not nachos?

What are you doing? Les asks.

The layers. It's layered like lasagna.

I love Mexican lasagna, he says. And this is one of the best I've ever had.

You hate nachos, Marlene says.

Who hates nachos? No one hates nachos. Nachos are delicious.

These aren't nachos, Josie insists.

Right, Marlene says. Because of the layers.

Quiet resets the room.

I'm wondering, Marlene starts again. How many layers makes it not nachos? Four? five?

Goddammit, Les says.

I'm just amazed to learn that no one has ever thought of layered nachos.

This isn't the time for your word games.

I'm in a playful mood.

Les's fork falls heavily on his plate.

Careful with those plates, she warns.

I'm sorry, Josie says. Do you want me to make you something else?

Oh, please, God, no.

I think it's great, Les says. The crew makes Mexican lasagna sometimes.

That's right, the crew, Marlene says. Which reminds me: Are you quitting or not? You've had enough time to think about it.

He has no chance to reply.

I knew it, she says. The only thing Stray can't stray from are his boyfriends on the boat.

I can't leave them shorthanded on short notice and you know it.

How about you? Marlene asks Josie.

I just feel sorry for you at this point.

You feel sorry for *me*? And what plans do *you* have to ride off into the sunset when you leave here?

I don't know yet. I haven't decided. Maybe I'll travel. Maybe to Arizona.

Maybe you'll go back to Bill?

Josie doesn't answer.

Boy, are you two damaged, Marlene laughs. You think *I'm* cracked—my idea for the three of us to stay down here together, you think *that's* twisted. But you know what's twisted? Long game, Les, who survives fishing? You know the answer and you still don't care. And you. Marlene turns to Josie again. The Villas? Really? Give me a break. I'm the only rational one at this table. Here we have a chance. Together, we can be OK. Why is that so hard to see?

Josie can decide what's best for herself, Les says.

Clearly, she can't.

She doesn't mean that, he says to Josie.

Of course I do.

If she doesn't want to stay, you can't make her.

I'll sure as hell try.

She's not our child, Les snaps. A child.

Listen to him, Josie, Marlene says. Can you hear it too? All that desperation? Anything to rewrite history, isn't that true, babe? No amount of positive or protective undoes the fact that you were never home. You were never home. You were never home.

What happened to her wasn't my fault.

How do you know?

I wasn't here.

Exactly.

How can we possibly have a life down here, Marlene?

Tell me it's my fault. Just tell me finally. Just say it out loud.

You can't even walk out to the driveway.

And you can't even say Angie's name.

Marlene launches her plate across the room, the ceramic shattering against the wall.

Just tell me, she says. If being gone makes you innocent, who's the only one left to blame?

The three of them are still.

At the window, frozen twigs of lilac rap.

Josie breaks the silence.

Les saved my life, she says.

He straightens in his chair, crossing his arms.

I'm embarrassed to even admit it. I don't know how it happened. I was partying with a bunch of his fishing crew at this hotel. Les wasn't there at the time we shot up. But the world slipped away and I found myself visiting rooms in my mind I never knew existed. I must've been out for a while because when I woke up it was morning. And Les was looking down over me. His buddies were going to let me die. Les made them call an ambulance. Then he shot me full of Narcan. And presto change-o rearrange-o, I was back. Staring up into his face. That's when I came to your apartment. Well, after I ran away from the hospital.

Marlene starts to say something and Josie interrupts her.

I don't want to talk about Bill right now. I'm talking about you two. My grandma used to call people's pain their darkness. She'd say you got to abide with your darkness as if it were a scared child that wakes up in the middle of the night and needs to be walked back down to bed. Nobody can do it for you, she'd say. You got to do it for yourself. You got to do it for the people you care about. You got to walk the darkness down. You're too good and too kind not to try.

Kind is never enough, Marlene says.

What about love? Josie asks.

Love is never enough.

MARLENE OPENS THE door to their bedroom and closes it behind her. Les, who's packing his bag to leave, looks up. They stare at each other across the room. She reads his reticence and his rage. He switches off the lamp to shut her out. The room goes dark. After dinner, Marlene remained in her chair until the candles burned down and sputtered out. She knew what had come over her at dinner, what always came over her. She was a fitful puppet of her own petulance. She'd gone too far this time. She didn't want Les to disappear under angry circumstances again. She's certain she didn't deserve Josie's well-intentioned words either.

The wind drives the rain into the windowpanes.

Thunder cracks outside.

A second later, lightning.

They look at each in the briefly lit room.

Don't go, she says.

Why's it always so mean with you?

I'm sorry.

Why's it always phrased without softness or patience, like you used to with her?

I'm sorry.

Thunder again.

The room takes shape with lightning a second time.

Marlene doesn't know what's come over her, but she's walking toward Les.

Her heart hammers against the rack of her chest bones.

She finds him in the darkness, pulling him to floor, their scared figures fumbling against each other as they strip off each other's clothes. It's over quick. Les's body seizes, Marlene under him, her thighs quivering. They fall asleep on the rug beneath a blanket they pull from the bed, and they discover each other again at some timeless hour. The storm has passed by then. The night is complete, solid, voluminous. Sight fails them. A hand finding a face, fingers grasping flesh, a moan rising from a mouth, are forms spontaneously sculpted.

THIRTEEN

My face was buried between her legs, right? Mouth dry, head dull, fingers on overdrive. My heart beating with wild bursts. Hoover's hand taps his chest at a quick, steady pace. He stands in front of Les's cutting station, face faintly bruised, hair windswept, killing the last bit of time before the first haul. The dredges are already down. We'd just smoked a joint, too, he says, so between the weed and white, I was shut in like a bad trip. All these quick thoughts just rushing me: Should a heart beat this fast? A hand cramp this bad? Also jaw ache? Slow up. Yank on that leash. That's it. Nice rhythm. Also, tongue. Don't lap like dog at bowl, Coke Dick. Move in circles. Spell out alphabet. Mouth dry. Would guzzle fishbowl, so thirsty, would slurp from toilet with straw. Need break. Need cigarette. Fingers reek of smoke. Got to be unsanitary. Can she get cancer secondhand this way? Secondhand! Secondhand, genius! Forearm burning. Switch to left.

They steamed out over three days this trip, the sky opening the farther east they traveled. The wind up, sea molten. The crew stripped down to their board shorts and long-sleeve tees, enthusiastic for gusts blowing fifteen out of the south. The optimism on deck was contagious until they heard word that this would be Stray's last ride.

Les took a bus up from Destiny the day after the storm, leaving Marlene the truck, and when he first got on board, Alright called him to the wheelhouse. Hoover and Booby were there too. Chain of command, alright? he said. A captain can't trust his mate, he can't do his job. Booby is good with Hoover and Monk, so I'm good with Hoover and Monk. Jesus, please us, we've been sitting on the sidelines for two weeks after the steering column fiasco and the nor'easter. Bygones be bygones, ladies. Kiss cheeks and focus up. Lutz already warned me: If we don't catch fish this trip, the coin is coming out of our own purses.

Les couldn't help himself. He quit right then.

Details of what Hoover did to Ethan spread quickly across the boat.

Now Les looks on from the hatch of the cutting room. Monk sits cross-legged on deck, camo-print shades concealing his eyes. He's captivated by Hoover's monologue. John Wayne, at the rail, silently seethes. He refuses to even talk to Les at this point. China babysits him while pretending not to, making sure John Wayne doesn't string Hoover up from the flounder nets. Les wonders what the boat will amount to without him. He wonders what he will amount to without the boat. Most of his life he's relied on the extremes of fishing. The punishing work and the self-annihilating exhaustion. The boisterousness of the crew and the quiet hours alone. Tasks that drive him relentlessly into himself and those merciful others that lift his eyes to the silent sea and permit him to become a passing witness to grandeur. He doesn't want his final haul to be steeped in so much doubt. The day is a fierce, burning blue, achingly clear.

Booby comes up behind him in the cutting room.

Maximum damage on the way out? That's the plan?

Something like that.

What happened to peace on the boat?

Your nephew, Les says.

They turn to Hoover.

Bad thoughts. Slow thoughts, he continues. Slooooooooow. Must still heartbeat with rail of Vicodin. Handful of Tylenol PM and a belly bath of crystal clear vodka. Cold as creek water. Wait, no. No, no. No downers. Shouldn't sleep, leaving in the A.M. Only a few more hours until departure. Another bump be nice. Bedtime bump. Ha-ha. Help play through till morning. Captain won't know. Captain won't care. Done it before. Everybody has. Just like Stray's old man. Don't go like Stray's old man. Do better than Stray's old man. Fuck Stray's old man. Also, fuck Stray!

The boat slows, engine idles, wet lines shrieking.

The boom cranks up the drags from the ocean floor.

John Wayne starts toward the hatch where Les and Booby stand.

Les is eager for a word from him, some sign of reconciliation or understanding.

John Wayne speaks to Booby instead.

Imagine if you could see that fuckup with two working eyes, he says.

Les smiles.

John Wayne keeps moving.

The dredges break the surface water.

Then, after prep over, sleep, sleep, sleep. Sleep seventy hours straight, just curl up in warm bunk with full stomach, air conditioner blasting, and dream. Best sleep always after binge. Permission to do nothing. Permission to power down and recharge. Oh, no, power down, power down! Also, mouth latched on. Clit is not a pacifier, Fuck Head. Lost rhythm. Losing her? Not moving. Asleep? Or worse, faking sleep? Yes, awake. See whites of eyes. Calm down, slow down. Must bury face here, must crawl inside and keep warm . . .

China clips up portside, Booby starboard, the two chain mesh scoops swinging on deck.

From out of the dredges spill massive piles of scallops.

Hoover raises his hands as if he himself just dropped the bounty onboard.

. . . Must curl up and live forever in the *sweat meat.*

Monk erupts in applause and Hoover takes a bow.

They are out five days, fish hold a quarter full, news of weather kicking up over the VHF in the wheelhouse, when Monk collapses into the pile. He and Hoover have been shooting dope in the lazarette compartment beside Les's cutting station—a location they appeared to enjoy as a taunt. Hoover continued to carry his weight, but Monk got sloppy, moving slower and slower, wavering in the heat over the pile, savaging the scallops.

Les is picking next to him when Monk's legs buckle.

Every monkfish across deck snaps its jaws shut in sequence.

Les tries to roll him onto his back, but he's too heavy. A fish near Monk's face kicks its tail angrily. Les tries again, heaving Monk hard by the shoulder, rolling him over with difficulty. The rest of the crew, just arriving, turn away, gasping in horror. A patch of Monk's stubbled cheek, clenched in the fish's shark teeth, tears from his face. Monk Man does not stir.

CAPTAIN CALLS A meeting an hour after they bandage Monk and put him to bed.

The hell is happening on my boat? he says.

Captain glares at Booby, who's been roused for his night shift at the helm.

We need to tighten up, alright?

We need to turn the boat around, Hoover says.

No way, China says. That'll fuck up another run.

Then call the Coast Guard to grab Monk.

Injury ain't life-threatening, Alright says.

It's Stray's fault. He tore his cheek off on purpose.

Hoover lunges at Les.

John Wayne intercepts him, throws Hoover against the wall.

He wraps his hands around his throat.

Booby rams his shoulder into John Wayne, tries to throw him off-balance.

China shoves his elbow into the old man's ribs and Booby stumbles back.

You're finished! Booby yells, pointing at China, fingers trembling. You're done!

Fuck you, old man! China shouts back. You did this.

Hoover, turning red, claws at John Wayne's hands.

How's helpless feel? John Wayne says.

Enough, Captain says. That's enough.

John Wayne doesn't relent.

I'm asking for Ethan. He wants to know. How's helpless feel?

Let him go. Now, alright?

John Wayne releases Hoover, who falls to the ground gasping.

We're coming apart at the seams out here, Captain says, scanning the crew, holding his disdain longest for Booby. We'll sort this shit out back home, you hear? Past is past for the time being. We're already down a man, for crying out loud. Weather coming, too, so we'll need to switch to a single dredge. But screw it, man, we double up shifts, pick up the pace. That way we don't fuck up another run, like China said. We head home with enough cargo to earn a proper check. Other option is turn back and take a huge hit again. That'll make it three trips in a row we come up short. That ain't my way, I'll tell you that. Lutz won't be happy with any one of us. He looks around to a silent galley. Onshore, all you sissies ever complain about is needing money and out here all you ever want to do is hightail it home. A couple more days, dammit. A couple more days, alright?

THE FINGER-PAINTED SUNSET fades black, shaded over by clouds sweeping up out of the south. An eerie intermingling of distant roars and the boat's mechanical thrum. Next, the water goes dark, lit only by sheets of quivering lightning advancing on the wind. A big sea rolls in with the storm. The wind licks the waves that crest the rail. The sounds of them crashing on deck drown the drone of the engine. Rain like static in the bright beams of the floodlights. The crew, working from one dredge, cut and bag as fast as they can. Les out on the stern, John Wayne, China, and Hoover all in the covered station. Booby up in the wheelhouse, cutting in the captain's trough, baskets lifted up to him from the deck. Alright sleeps. Monk still out cold. Les keeps his eyes down, his slicker soaked from the wind ripping off the sea. A headlamp lights his work.

The boat halts suddenly.

Les is thrown to his knees.

The cables flex and tighten, screech to a stop in the drawn pullies.

Base bolts groan as the winch jolts.

The boat turns side-to then hard over, bow rearing up like a horse protesting its reins.

The dredge is stuck to something on the bottom, Les knows, expecting the wire cable to snap, the tension too great to hold. But the cable slackens instead, starts letting out line as the boat steams forward now, moored to the seafloor.

Les races to the wheelhouse, finds Booby cussing at himself.

Captain rushes in next. What the fuck?

I ran over a wreck.

How'd you manage that?

I was cutting at my trough.

Why the hell were you out there?

Trying to make up for losing Monk.

You dumb shit. How bad is it?

Dredge caught, Les says. We're letting out line.

What happened to the brake stop?

Wasn't set.

Jesus fucking Christ.

I'm sorry, Captain, Booby says. I should've seen the structure down there.

Radio our coordinates. Wake everybody up. Prep the immersion suits just in case. Go check the engine room, Stray. Make sure there's no water getting in. And you—he turns to Booby—I'm backing this bitch up until we're right on top of the dredge. We'll be able to free it up from there. Stand guard at the haul-back station. I need eyes as I shift into reverse. The sea ain't going our way and it's as black as ass back there.

Booby jumps to the haul-back station, Les to the engine room.

On the way down the ladder, the boat slamming into the troughs of waves, he misses a rung and drops the ten feet, landing hard on his tailbone. The pain shoots up to his neck. By the time he hobbles to the engine room, John Wayne has already sealed the hatch.

He looks Les up and down, sees him walking gingerly.

You fall?

Les nods.

Life is tough, but it's tougher if you're stupid.

Les smiles and starts to say something.

I know, John Wayne says. It's OK.

I'm sorry I didn't tell you.

I wouldn't've told me either.

Well, why the hell you been ignoring me this trip?

I'm pissed, that's why. Plus you're leaving.

We'll still see each other.

What does that mean? You breaking up with me? Course we'll still see each other. I'm happy for you, John Wayne says. Happier for Marlene, so we're clear.

He's about to say more when an alarm blares.

Shouts draw them quickly to deck, where bushels of scallops have tipped out of the baskets and now swirl in the water, slip out the scuppers, all those dollars flushed back to sea. A tall face crashes over the stern and the boat lists dangerously. The water gurgles and disappears into the lazarette. The hatch was left open, the compartment flooding. The ass of the boat begins to drop.

They all climb to the wheelhouse.

Who's been going down into the lazarette? Alright's eyes stop on Hoover. I ought to throw you off my boat this instant. You and that piece of shit Monk. Where is he, anyway? Booby, just then reaching the wheelhouse, tells Captain that Monk won't wake up. Won't what? Are you kidding me? You're useless, Booby. He turns to John Wayne, China, and Les. Cut the dredge loose and seal the compartment. We ain't gonna sink with a belly full of water but we need to get off this wreck. Then we can bring the boat to fair wind. Captain sees them hesitate. I'm not asking for volunteers, sons. It's a three-man job. And you're the only three I can trust.

They slip into immersion suits, descend to the deck together.

John Wayne lights the welding torch.

Give it here, Les says.

Let somebody else be the hero for once, John Wayne says.

He rips the torch from John Wayne.

Get clear once you seal the lazarette.

I'm coming with you, Stray, China says.

Les nods.

They inch toward the pulley, hands on the portside rail stabilizing them, China just behind Les, hauling the gas hose. Les climbs up the A-frame, clips his waist to the beam, shortens the flame to blue, and applies the heat to the wire cable. China clips up to the beam just below Les's feet. John Wayne crawls to the lazarette and peers down.

A wave lifts over the bulwark, hitting Les and China hard, knocking John Wayne starboard.

They hug the boat, hold tight to withstand the list.

They wait for another wave to crash.

The boat sways as thousands of pounds of water rush aboard.

The listing stops and John Wayne wades out to the lazarette and seals the compartment.

But Les is unable to burn through the wire.

The cable keeps slackening and tightening with the roll of the sea.

The winds and waves in his ear, Les spits out at China: Winch, slack, pulley.

China gives a thumbs-up, drops the hose, unclips from the beam, and kicks his way to the winch up near the cutting room. He flips the switch. The cable, taut a few seconds later, starts snapping with each strand Les burns through. *Pop.* Les yells for John Wayne and China to clear out. They give another thumbs-up and turn to the hatch. From out of the cutting room a shadow emerges. It's Monk, in T-shirt and board shorts, stumbling onto the deck like a soldier stunned by an explosion, his hand peeling the bandage off his face. *Pop.* John Wayne yells at him to get back inside. Monk doesn't listen. He falls to a knee when the ship lists. They hustle to him as a massive wave smacks the deck.

The torch falls from Les's grip.

He reaches desperately into the darkness.

He grasps the hose just as the boat rolls to starboard.

The A-frame rising, he sees John Wayne and China below, each with a hand on Monk, another on the rail, unable to let go of either.

When the boat settles, they watch the sea gather again behind Les.

Les guesses that they're going to make a jump to the cutting room.

John Wayne and China hold on for another wave, getting down the timing.

The fire in the torch has been extinguished and Les doesn't even bother relighting.

He cannot look away.

They time it as best as they can.

Between waves, they gather up Monk by his arms and leap toward the hatch.

Monk doesn't budge.

He grips the rail tighter, screaming with terror.

John Wayne jerks him free but slips hard, hitting the back of his head in the fall.

Monk only collapses, curling into a ball.

The boat turns fully broadside to a lashing swell.

The wave surprises Les, knocks him from distraction, it hits his back so hard.

China has grabbed Monk by the coveralls.

He's dragging him across deck toward the cutting room.

John Wayne struggles to regain his balance.

He stands tall before falling again to one knee.

He fingers the blood dripping down his neck.

He's too far from the rail and too far from the hatch.

His eyes turn to the rush of water.

There's time to raise a hand halfway, time to open his mouth as if to swallow up the wave.

The boat rolls to starboard again.

Les searches the settling spray.

The boat swings back to port.

Les's sight lines finally clear.

China and Monk are safe in the cutting room.

John Wayne is nowhere to be found.

John Wayne is gone.

Les sobs, his muscles frail and failing.

He must put the flame back on the cable. He must gather the strength to relight the torch and keep at his assignment. Each second John Wayne slips farther and farther away, but Les has to free the boat first. He sparks the torch and applies the flame. *Pop.* In John Wayne's eyes swam the cries of terrified men. In them Les also saw the younger version of his friend: small freckled nose soon to broaden, toothy grin he learns to cover with his top lip until he can grow a mustache, baby fat that would later harden and bulge. *Pop.* They had a song back in grade school that they'd chant together while running barefoot through the street. It was the same song he used to put his daughter to sleep those rare nights he was home.

Wind from the east, fish bite the least;
Wind from the west, fish bite the best;
Wind from the north, few set forth;
Wind from the south blows bait in their mouth.

Stars spray everywhere, and in these endless, powerless seconds she's with him again: on the Ferris wheel, fireworks overhead. She clutches Dolphy, still refusing to give it up. He failed to save his daughter and now he's failed to save his friend. The full devastation of this reality bears down on him. *Pop.* The final wire cable snaps from the flame—the boat free of the dredge—and Les unclips himself, jumps down off the A-frame, races across deck, and leaps over the rail and into the waves.

FOURTEEN

Several nights ago, Marlene woke to the sound of Josie's voice. It was late, early morning almost. She snuck downstairs, saw her speaking into the hidden phone, surmising Bill was on the other end. The next day she brought home a second landline, plugged it in upstairs after the lights were out, and began listening to them talk. The conversations run long, sometimes charged with silence, and in these moments Marlene recognizes a loss that feeds the threshing flame of desire. She knows that Josie is leaving, that she won't stay in Destiny much longer, and she's dismayed that Josie might still succumb to Bill's witchy words and ways.

Marlene paces her bedroom, hand over the mouth of the cordless receiver.

Right on time, Bill says.

Yeah? Josie says.

Yeah, baby, I was born at 3:00 A.M.

What did you do for the big day?

We had an office party.

Who catered?

A certain somebody used to make me a cake.

Stop.

OK, if you say so. Have you given any more thought to coming home?

I might go visit my mom.

What a life, he says. Instant coffee and microwaved food, sweatpants and tube socks, La-z-Boys and daytime TV, soft packs of 100s, cavities, clinics, single-wides, paychecks pissed away on scratch-offs and Big Gulps.

The last letter I got from her she sounded good.

Josie, baby, desperation is a thing you've known your whole life. The stench you get off desperate folks, that smell, people get a lungful, thinking, *Poor thing*. They wonder why that person doesn't do something more about the reek coming off them. Why they don't change their life. They don't know that smell is on purpose. It's meant to repel them, to keep people back. Your mom hasn't lost that stench, sweets. She might want you near for a minute, but she's built to turn you off. From the moment you were born, her body was saying: *Get back, Josephine. Get back. Stay back*. You know, I used to know a guy that shot up with Tabasco.

You did not.

That's how bad he wanted to keep people away.

Josie laughs.

You still love me, don't you? he asks.

She says nothing.

He waits.

He has the patience of a cat.

You know what? Don't answer. I love you enough for both of us. And I've been wanting to tell you something important. I always hoped to move on from The Villas. Men should take some chances in life, have the nerve. If you got nothing else going for you, at least have that. Maybe I'll regret it, walking away. But

I'll be relieved too. I don't give a shit about The Villas. I don't care about myself. I care about us.

Marlene hears something in the bathroom.

She walks over, still listening to the call.

Remember the whoopie pies from the One Stop? he asks.

Don't.

Nice memory.

You can't attack me with nice memories.

There's a banging inside the toilet. Something jumps.

Marry me, he says. How's that?

Nothing, still, from Josie.

Let me come get you, he pleads. Where are you?

Marlene opens the top and screams into the phone, slamming the lid closed.

She hears Josie barreling up the stairs.

She ends the call, slips the phone into the wastebasket.

Marlene, what's going on? Where are you?

Josie darts into the bathroom.

What were you doing on the phone? Josie asks.

Don't you dare.

Marlene stares Josie down, then turns back to the toilet.

She cracks open the lid for her to see.

A frog, clinging to the edge of the bowl, springs, hits the lid, and splashes back down.

Marlene slams it shut once more.

Gross. Flush it, Josie says.

I'm not flushing it. What if it drowns?

What, you're going to reach in and pick it up?

No. Maybe. What about like a container? Scoop it out?

Just flush it.

You think it's an American bullfrog?

I don't know.

Tell me if it's one of them we were reading about. You've seen them before.

Does it have a yellow throat?

I don't know, Josie, I didn't stick my face into the toilet to check.

Well, open it up again.

Marlene lifts the lid a little higher this time.

They both peer into the toilet.

Yes, definitely a yellow throat, Marlene says.

And a green upper lip.

What the hell? Can you believe it?

But it's so small. They're supposed to be huge.

Maybe it's a baby.

The bullfrog leaps again and Marlene closes the lid too late.

Josie yelps.

Marlene chases the frog as it escapes the bathroom, through the hallway, down the stairs, and onto the damask sofa in the sitting room, trailing wet webbed prints along the way. She finally traps it on the floor, inside an antique pitcher she pulled from the mantel.

Together, she and Josie release the frog into the backyard.

In the kitchen Marlene washes her hands.

Josie watches her from a stool.

The phone she unlocked from the desk sits on the island.

They both look at it.

I'm not going to marry him, Josie says.

Why have you been talking to him?

I'm testing him. Josie corrects herself. I'm testing myself.

I can't lose you back to Bill.

You're not losing me back to him. But you are going to lose me.

I'll drive you to the airport right now. I'll buy your ticket. You can fly far away.

I don't have energy for this tonight. Let's talk about it in the morning.

I'm not tired.

You should try and sleep. It's late.

I'm going to take a walk.

It's cold outside.

Who asked you to come?

Jesus, fuck.

They make their way along the tree line, between the pond and the eastern rim of the field. Little is said between them. Marlene finds herself invigorated to be out in the briskness and the beauty. The long drifting furrows in the land flood with light. At the property's edge a bare thicket of gray poplar is illuminated. Shards of a shattered moon swim languidly on the canal. They make a hard left and come upon a footpath that veers from the water and the land starts to rise. Marlene leads them uphill to a DO NOT ENTER sign. She hops the gate, Josie following. The slope rises steeply for some time and then plateaus. At the top, Marlene waits for Josie to catch up. Sprawling before them is a long stretch of barren, cracked earth, the arid terrain of an inhospitable desert, not the damp sand of a coastal land. Josie looks across the expanse, traces the intersecting network of cracks, which from these heights appear to extend all the way to the sea.

What the hell, Josie says. Where are we?

When the Army Corp of Engineers dredged the canal about eighty years ago, they dumped the spoils right here. That's what we are standing on, where this little mountain comes from.

How deep are these cracks?

God, who knows? Watch your step.

They trek carefully across and at the other end descend onto a hillside covered with giant phragmites. The fluorescent tips hover disembodied from their stalks, a floating canopy of feathery lanterns. They take another turn at a dirt path, following it through an old-growth forest that creeps right up to the dunes, where they hear the sound of waves and emerge onto the beach. Several branch lengths of driftwood, sculpted by the sea, are scattered ashore, smooth as fossils. Josie lies down on the sand while Marlene sits upright, her eyes on the ocean and the bright tabletop clouds.

Josie twirls blades of beach grass.

The crash of the waves reverberates in Marlene's ears.

Marlene sees Josie shivering.

She takes off her jacket, lays it over her.

Marlene turns her head to gaze down the beach but also to hold Josie in her periphery.

Do you think I could have a life down here again?

You're all right here, Josie says. It's all right.

But do you think I could have a life?

Yes.

I don't trust that kind of certainty.

Tell me what happened, then, and I'll tell you what I think.

The waves break over the rips a hundred yards offshore.

Waves that far out usually mean there's been a storm at sea, Marlene says.

She feels a swelling inside her, a pang of despair, as Les comes to mind.

Me, now you, Josie says.

Marlene reaches for a cigarette but they're in her coat.

Josie sparks her Merit.

Marlene accepts the smoke and takes a long drag.

Angie had this stuffed animal, she begins. A dolphin. Les won it for her at a carnival. When he was gone, which was all the time, you couldn't get it out of her hands. I was actually getting worried about her, the way she took it everywhere. The way she ignored other kids. It was her only friend. Or maybe she just missed her dad. I brought her to see someone once. Some counselor. She assured me there was nothing to worry about. Called Angie an extroverted introvert. She loved to perform but only ever wanted the stuffed animal and her parents to be the audience.

The beaches were overrun, Marlene goes on. That's how I remember the day of the week. A Tuesday. People had escaped to the coast because of this insane heat wave passing through the region. Les was out scalloping—surprise—so I brought Angie down. We pulled my dad away from his house projects, and the four of us—my dad, my mom, me, and Angie—went to one of the crowded beaches, hoping maybe Angie would find some kids to play with. But by noon the index was through the roof and she was just sitting with Dolphy beneath an umbrella, so we decided to beat the heat back home again.

My mom and I made lunch inside while my dad continued laying stone for a footpath, Angie his little helper. I remember looking at them through the window. He kept giving her tasks, sending her to the barn to bring him a different tool, usually the wrong one. I was just relieved that she wasn't holding Dolphy at that moment. She'd forgotten about it, you know? Part of me even hoped she'd left the damn thing at the beach.

Inside, my mom and I were in an argument. They wanted to retire and that meant I would either need to take over the lumber company or they were going to sell it. This wasn't the first time we'd had this conversation. I'd been their bookkeeper for years, and I knew the business wasn't doing as well as it should, but still

I was asking for more time again. My mom said they already had a buyer. I was so angry—at my parents for making me realize that I was actually going to leave Les, and at Les for knowing this was going to happen and doing nothing to stop it. Then, Angie was there with us in the kitchen, looking for an audience as always. I was pretty good about ignoring her when she annoyed me, but I yelled at her that time. Whatever I said must have been bad because my mom would hardly speak to me after Angie stormed out. I don't even remember which direction she left the kitchen.

We thought she was hiding at first. She'd done that before at a department store. I figured she was mad at me for snapping at her. After a while we started to worry, thinking maybe she got lost in the woods or found something dangerous to play with in the barn. Maybe she'd gone to the pond to cool off? Maybe the hammock for shade? Maybe she'd walked down the block to see the alpaca farm, the funny animals that always amused her? We yelled and yelled her name. We split up to search separately. I walked down the street. My dad policed the field. My mom stayed home in case Angie showed up. We eventually called the cops. They came quick but took forever getting down the details. Then, when they were leaving, one of them spotted her on the way back to the cruiser. We'd thought of so many scenarios except the one where she'd accidently locked herself in the backseat of my mom's car, where she'd left Dolphy. God, it was so hot that day! She passed out from the heat just a few feet away, right there in the driveway, roasting in that oven for hours . . .

Marlene trails off.

She waits for the tears to come.

The tears do not come.

Moisture has settled over the dune grass Josie twirls.

She grasps two bunches, skims the dew from the blades.

She reaches out her hands and wets Marlene's cheeks.

Well? Marlene asks.

Well what?

Do you think I can have a life down here again?

Josie is quiet.

Yes, she finally says.

She hesitated too long.

Marlene's already up, starting the quarter mile home.

Josie follows a step behind.

They walk down the middle of the road, bare trees looming overhead.

Day breaks pink in the visible strip of sky.

At the house, Marlene walks up the gravel driveway.

She halts at the spot.

Here's her little girl, curled up in the footwell, desperate for shelter, for shade. Marlene watches herself open the door. The ghastly heat escapes. She lifts Angie up into her arms, clutches her daughter, sobbing into her ear, implores her to breathe, to live, one breath, just that first breath. God, give her the strength for one small breath.

Angie, cradling Dolphy, sleeps.

Marlene's cell phone rings inside the house and they turn their eyes to the front door. The ringing ends but then begins again. Josie starts walking to the entrance, Marlene on her heels, the hour and recurrence of the calls alarming them. Josie's pace quickens, as does Marlene's, until they are nearly running. First through the door, Josie finds the cell and hands it to Marlene, who grasps that it's Alright on the satellite phone when she sees the call show up UNKNOWN.

FIFTEEN

At the age of eighteen, when he first started scalloping full-time, Les suffered from sleep paralysis. The condition is not uncommon among fishermen. It lasted only a few years, fading away as the work-rest cycle on the trawler normalized. Back then he went down easy, but dreams would float up fast, mischievous and terrifying dreams from which he would attempt to will himself awake so urgently that his mind would come alert though his body still slept. At first, confused by this disharmony, he hallucinated a presence sitting on his chest, pinning him down as his mind screamed and flailed and wept until he bolted upright in the berth. But as the condition advanced, the dreams evolved. The presence disappeared and the time it took Les to wake lengthened. He could be trapped inside himself for what seemed like hours. In that paralyzed state, he would feel himself falling down, down, down into a depthless sea. Body still, mind wild, he watched the light near the surface of the water wither as he dropped deeper into a blackness so vast that it used the world for a reservoir.

That is what it feels like when Les loses consciousness over the hollows of the sea.

Despite his immersion suit, the cold stunned his limbs once he dove into the water. He swam with desperation, with purpose, swam for survival, for warmth, restricted and protected by the buoyant neoprene. He swam toward the blinking light on John Wayne's suit, away from the boat, powering through the swell, churning onward. He imagined his body like a machine, the kind that recycled its byproduct as fuel. When his limbs grew tired, he swam for rest. When his breath was short, he swam for air. When dread crippled his mind, he swam for courage, for faith. He swam and swam until he ground to a halt, lungs burning, and stopped to take his bearings. The light on John Wayne's suit had vanished. The trawler was nowhere to be seen.

He rested for a moment before sinking into a fear that sputtered like his breath.

Panic surged and he swam again, this time with wasteful, failing strokes.

He changed directions impulsively, his entire body filled with unexpected movement.

Sucking air, he vomited from the salt water and exertion.

He was forced again to rest, to calm down, held up in the swell by the suit's flotation.

Les did not lose time, but the hours that passed took on the effect of sleep. There was blackness above, blackness beyond, the sea a glistening obsidian. Rain poured down relentlessly. Cold set in, creeping up from the toes, slowed the flow of blood. Stilting his thoughts. Mind lurching. Lunging? Lurching.

He swam for clarity. Only a few strokes and stopped.

Spasms in his feet, his legs. His mind. Shivering. He couldn't feel his fingers. *Fangers*, as his father said the word. Old man dead in all this *wudder* for *water*. Locals used *yuh* for *yes*. Marlene spent a year trying to get their daughter to say it right. Daughter. Her name. Angie.

Angie.

Angie.

She stretched out the *s* in protest of Marlene's correction. A big joke by the end. All of them laughing at the table. More milk? Essssss. Do you love your papa? Esssssss. What color is the sky? Esssssss.

His mind sank deeper into the blackness.

Shouldn't he be detaching by now? Looking down on himself from above, heart swollen with sympathy for his own misunderstandings, for the wrong way of living, all that misplaced fear that the women he loves were destined to abandon him—mother, daughter, wife? But he wasn't a victim. And he certainly wasn't a hero. He had abandoned Angie as his mother had abandoned him. He distanced himself from Marlene as his father had distanced himself as well. He missed so much, was gone too long. It was Marlene who cleaned up after the birthday parties, helped her through sicknesses, potty training, school shopping, her voice the one that penetrated the womb, the stimuli that whispered to Angie's senses: *Grow, grow.* It was Marlene who read books aloud, taking on different personalities for every character, igniting her theatricality, enchanting her with the outdoors, too, teaching her trees, teaching her birds—all while Les preferred to be at sea. When she was born, he cherished the new light pressing out from inside him. But he also set its confines strictly, scared of what havoc that kind of limitlessness could wreak on a person. So he ran, again and again, afraid of shattering, doubting his ability to hold within himself any more love. His heart suddenly broke realizing that he couldn't give Angie one pure moment of utter attention right now. He couldn't find John Wayne out here, either, so they weren't both so alone at the end. He couldn't give Marlene the apology she deserved. He'd never really given up anything for her, never made an honest sacrifice in favor of her happiness. He felt sorry for her too. She was the one left behind. Again. But none of that was right, either, he sensed. Here, adrift, the waves rocking him in the cradle of the sea, the blackness everywhere, edging in his vision, there's no judgment. There's only now: his body losing warmth, heat escaping. He was taking on the cold, becoming the sea. Soon it would all be the same temperature, all the same ocean, all in a single, dispersing second.

Esssssss, he said.

Esssssss, the water whispered back.

He was hushed to sleep, the blackness complete.

Then a sudden burst of light, and his chest is on fire.

His mouth shoots open, lungs gasping.

He wakes on his back, senses intertwined.

Wind whips noiselessly in his ears.

He shivers from the chill of the cold, quiet moon.

The great weight of the blanket smothers him in an embrace.

Marlene attends to him in a white and orange flight helmet.

But it's not her, and he turns disappointed to the open bay.

He still might be dead, he thinks when he sees from above: the shore advancing on the sea, the night-dark waters turning luminescent in the shallows, the long white froth lines of the waves, the yellow banner of beach dotted green with dune grass, then the ribbons of the first flora—red cedars, golden rods, and bayberries—the changes in color and texture from this view like the layers of an early rock, as if time itself had been cored, logged, and splayed out before him—and then civilization emerges, all gridded and glowing. Before long the helicopter hovers over the hospital, the world becoming more recognizable the farther down he descends.

★ ★ ★

MARLENE LENGTHENS EACH of Les's digits along the sheet, straightening the knuckles. Her palm to the back of his hand, she applies pressure, pushing down his fingers as fully as the safety restraints around his wrists allow. Next she sweeps the grime from beneath his nails with a curved blade before clipping them. She soaks the right hand in a plastic pitcher filled with warm water, lemon juice, and baking soda. The lemon juice she procured from packets in the cafeteria, the baking soda from the nurses' fridge in the break room. Here, she would have moved to the left hand, but the bandages around his pinky and first finger, amputated above the middle joints from hypothermia, hold her back.

The drive up was excruciating. Marlene remained white-knuckled on the wheel as the mile markers ticked by and the truck raced the route home. She was consumed by anger. He never heeded her caution that something would happen to him one day at sea. The crew too. No one had listened. What about their jokes now? What about their stupid nicknames and Never-land antics now? In moments of despair, times when she was drawn out of the trance of the road by the shock of his face gone white, she found herself veering from the instinct of bitterness toward another known path: mourning. No more would she hear him laugh in his sleep, no more would she hide notes in his window visor, no more would she let him hold her at night, warding off whatever fear continued to carve out new dark within him—habits of the past she thought she left behind.

By the time she arrived at the hospital, Les's medevac had long since landed, the rest of the crew still a day deep into the Atlantic. Marlene ran inside to the ICU, where she found Les asleep, PICC line fed into his veins, burns on his chest from the defibrillator shocking him back to life. Les was breathing on his own, a great sign, the doctor said. The upshot: What damage the cold had done to his organs they would know in the next few days. For now, he needed rest.

She does too.

She considers climbing into Les's bed, pulling out his piping, and folding in for a nap.

But there's Josie in the corner.

In the room, just as during the drive, her presence looms like a stranger's, which confuses Marlene because of how close she feels to Josie and how soon she knows Josie will leave. But the relief that Les is alive is all she has room for inside. She remembers one time as a young girl camping with her mother on their back lawn. She woke alone in the tent and climbed out to see the fire her mom had built for breakfast. It was morning, brisk, spring still touched by winter. She hasn't thought of this for years. She doesn't know why she's thinking of it now. Over the field beyond, which back then seemed as wide and majestic as a great valley, the sun rose, and the cover of shadow pulled off the land like a slow unveiling. She saw worry leave her mother's face as she watched, a change come over her, and Marlene turned her head back to the field, pretending to feel it too. Something is important until it is important no longer.

After the soak she uses a washcloth to wipe away the top layers of calluses. She massages Neosporin into the skin. Then, once absorbed, another coat, working the jelly into his pads with her thumbs in order to compel its properties downward. Last, she applies a moisturizing cream and proceeds to knead his palm, relax the muscles of his hand. Each gentle, exacting touch is an act of completion, an avowal of a tenderness she tries to project into him. She hasn't cared for his hands this way in years.

A nurse enters the room, informs her that Les's friends have just arrived.

There's anger back in Marlene.

But in the waiting room she stops short of berating the crew. She scans their faces—each of them hangdog, suffering in their way—and she draws in a short shock of breath when she doesn't see John Wayne among them.

Where is he?

What are you doing here? Hoover says.

Marlene turns around to see Josie, who's just come up behind her.

Go back to the room, Marlene says.

You know her?

Who's that? Booby says.

That's the bitch Stray got all bent out of shape about.

Where's John Wayne?

We couldn't find him, China says. He's lost.

Monk mumbles something.

He mumbles again, still unclear.

What the fuck is he saying? Alright says. Speak up.

Drooowned, Monk howls, his voice trembling in the long hollow vowel. Droooowned.

Quiet grips them. The first utterance of Monk's word sounded ambiguous, out of place. The repetition, though, acts strangely on them, stifling those who heard, forcing them into themselves as swiftly as the water that rushed John Wayne's lungs. Marlene doesn't know what's worse: imagining her friend dying a gruesome death or the gratitude she feels that it wasn't Les.

HIS FIRST DAY in the ICU, Les was out from sedation. The morphine kept him under, tubes fed him fluids, nurses came in and out, monitoring machines. In his mind, he remained in the blackness of the sea, which by the second day wasn't nearly as complete. Gray began to shade the borders of his mind and he would sometimes open his eyes, see the blur of Marlene busy at different tasks—Marlene touching his hands, Marlene talking to someone in the room, Marlene carrying something heavy that clings to her neck—almost always silhouetted by the blinding window light. He would slur a word even he couldn't fix to a thought and then drift back to sleep. On the third day, Les finally opens his eyes for good, sedation waning. His orientation spreads from the soreness of his chest to the ghosts of fingers to Marlene asleep in a chair, and he sees that it's been Ethan in her arms this whole time.

As he watches them sleep, Les gathers most of what happened on the boat: the cable freeing up the stern, Les diving overboard, John Wayne lost, the call to shore for a medevac and the helicopter, his hospital stay, Marlene by his bed.

He rolls to his side, careful not to disturb them.

He sees a note on the tray table, his name written in Marlene's hand.

He reaches for it, groans from the stiffness of his chest.

Marlene wakes.

They plunge into each other's eyes.

They wait for the other to make a noise.

Did they find him? he asks.

Marlene shakes her head.

Les looks at Ethan.

Does he know?

We took a walk out to the courtyard, she whispers. He hasn't left my arms since.

Josie, in the corner, stirs next.

Les sits up some.

Full house, he says.

Tell me about it.

He nods to the note.

You didn't break the door again, did you? he asks.

Marlene laughs, covering her mouth.

I didn't want you to be alone if you woke up and I wasn't here.

He opens the envelope.

The note reads: *Dinner tonight?*

He smiles.

His stomach growls loudly.

Is that a yes?

I'm so hungry I could eat my own fingers.

She laughs again.

Stop, she says. I'm not ready for them to wake up.

But Josie stirs for good and Ethan too.

Then it seems the stream of doctors and nurses will never end. They remove the restraints, change the dressing, ask him to raise his arm, wiggle his toes, check his pupils. There's a discussion about his heart, his blood, his urine output, his brain function. They mention meds, electrolytes, soft diets. And when they finally leave, the crew floods in. Les is surprised by how uplifted he feels to see them, heartened by the abundance of resilience he knows now fits into this small room. But he also detects that something central is missing, slipping away from him. Not John Wayne, whose absence overwhelms in a different way, but rather Marlene, her physical proximity, the distance he notices more acutely as she's forced behind the flow of visitors. Les observes her face betray the same desire to be near him. He holds their longing close.

MARLENE SITS IN the courtyard smoking a cigarette. After all the commotion in the room earlier today, Les fell back asleep. When he woke up again, his hand throbbed terribly. The nurse gave him something for the pain. Marlene suspects he'll be out until morning. She imagines he will feel more like himself by then. Overhead, the sky is streaked with dusk, patches of green dapple the trees, a murmuring of birds like an ink-smudged fingerprint. Yesterday she sat here with Ethan. John Wayne's sister had served as babysitter this past haul and she drove straight to the hospital after hearing the news, incapable of looking at the child in her backseat. They are still trying to track down Kathleen. No one wanted the task of explaining to the boy that his father was gone.

Your dad is with God, she told him, dabbing out a Merit.

We don't believe in God, he said, surprising her.

They watched a rabbit dash across the first grass and dive into a hole.

I see, she said. Your dad is with the bunnies.

He scooted close to her, buried his face into her elbow.

Now the boy was back with his aunt, and Marlene missed the weight of him in her arms.

She scratches out the cigarette, collects the smokes and lighter.

Josie comes up behind her.

She's packed what clothes she's accumulated the past few weeks into a grocery bag.

Marlene notes her calm.

Are you going to see Bill?

Yes.

Aren't you scared?

Of course I am. But I can't just run away. I need to tell him I'm leaving to his face.

He won't understand.

I'm not doing it for him.

Remember when you came over a couple months back, your hand broken? When you looked at me and said he never poked you in the eye?

I'm better now.

You can't go back to him.

I'm not. I'll tell him no and leave.

OK, Marlene says, unconvinced.

I hate to go like this.

It's time, though.

I'll stay if you need me.

No, I'll be fine.

OK, then, no big goodbyes, Josie says. I don't think either of us has the energy for that.

How should we do it, then?

Why don't we just pretend like you're dropping me off at college?

So now you play along?

A parting gift.

I'll have to pick up a hobby.

Other than hookers.

And natural disasters.

A sadness follows their banter.

Where are you going after? Marlene asks.

I'm going home. To my mom.

Marlene feels both deficient and relieved.

They hug each other.

How will we know you're safe?

I'll send you a postcard, Josie says, smiling. Say goodbye to Les.

I will.

And then Josie's gone.

Upstairs in the room, Marlene keeps her forehead pressed to the glass even though she watched Josie climb into a cab a half hour ago. She fights the fear that Josie will fall back into things with Bill. She imagines instead her going straight to the airport after leaving the motel. She hops the first flight out, no matter the destination, maybe Atlanta, maybe Memphis. She connects from there, hopscotching west a leg at a time: St. Louis, Dallas, Denver, Phoenix. There's a stop at the airport bar before boarding. The music in the place pulses with life. She orders something tropical, something sweet. She twists the same cocktail umbrella all the way across the continent to a separate sea. Marlene feels some freedom in her leaving, she admits to herself. She also notices the unease. There's nothing left in the way of Les whenever she's ready to turn back around.

THE MORNING IS an active one. Les wakes to another note from Marlene telling him that she's gone home to get some rest. When she returns, they'll talk, the note ends. He stays busy to forget the fit in his stomach brought on by that last line. He walks up and down the hallway to get his legs firing. He does wall squats and arms raises with a group of elderly patients. He swings by the waiting room looking for action. There's no crew, no Ethan, no Josie, no Marlene; the hospital has become quiet and lonely. Back in his room, he doesn't want to climb into bed, and the nurse permits him to rest in a chair by the window for a while. Looking out doesn't make him feel less anxious. The television doesn't help much either.

Marlene shows up around lunchtime.

Les is still in the chair.

He mutes the TV.

She sits on the foot of his bed.

He notices a weariness in her, the forward fall of her shoulders.

The ironic inflection and slight curve of her mouth are gone from the ends of sentences.

The silence stretches out, awkward and expectant.

I have this dream, Les says. The three of us are on the Ferris wheel just after I won Dolphy for her and there's this storm coming fast in the background. Big lightning, big sea. Your back's to it, so I'm the only one of us that sees it coming, senses the danger. And I know that I'm supposed to get Dolphy from her before it makes landfall. I know that if I don't, something terrible will happen to her. But she won't give it up. She won't hand it over. No matter how much I beg or how hard I pull, she won't let it go. And there's nothing I can do about it. The simplest thing to save her and I can't even do it. I have this other image that's related, I think. It comes to me regular too. From that first day down in Destiny when you took me out to the property. The grass is tall, the sun up, and you turn around and look at me. It's hard to even describe that look. Like you already possessed whatever it was you wanted out of life. Not things. I don't mean objects. I mean inside of you. Like the notion to judge yourself so harsh would never take root. And I have this rush of regret for not trusting that you. Like all I have to do to make everything OK again is to concede right then to that you.

Why didn't you?

Lasts, he says. Lasts. All the lasts people remind you of when you get married and have kids. Last months of freedom. Last night you'll party till sunrise. Last winter you'll beat down in Florida. Last time you'll ever go out to sea for weeks at a time, living a certain kind of life, one that sets you apart, that feels like you were born for it. Everyone telling you that it ends when you settle down. But when she was born . . . when *Angie* was born, the opposite of what everybody told me would happen happened. Nothing ended. Instead, the world was filled with firsts. First smile, first step, first word, first birthday, first grade. But that wasn't any better, either, because I feel like I mourned every day that way. Every day, every first, felt like a little death. It was all happening so fast and that scared the hell out of me. Then she was gone and my new world was filled with a different kind of firsts, the ghosts of them: first kiss, first love, first job. She would still be alive if I hadn't given her that toy or if we'd moved to Destiny. Or if you had just left me. What stopped you from leaving me?

It was never about firsts or lasts for me, Marlene says. It wasn't even about Angie. It was always about you, about trying to find some kind of balance with you, some kind of in between. At one moment you were Les, or trying to be, and the next you were Stray, which came easy. I guess I never understood you. I don't know if I ever really tried. So much pride and so much fear, only ever kind or cold, always with the extremes. I did know that the guilt of running away required that you keep running. But the *why* didn't make any sense. It still doesn't. Even after hearing you talk. I remember that day in Destiny different. Your palms were so coarse, they made my words, even my thoughts, sound silly to me. Your broken hands gave you some kind of authority over me, even though I was a few years older than you. Maybe that's why I worked on them when you were home, hoping they'd soften, hoping you'd see me and Angie and stay. Back then, I didn't leave because I was scared to raise her alone, even though I was doing it already. And now I haven't left because you're my punishment for not leaving sooner, the punishment for my indecision. I'm sure you blame me too. I was the one with her. I was the one on watch.

She takes a moment before going on.

When we lost her, it was like emptiness was suddenly this abundant thing. I did the grief groups. They taught us visualization techniques that were supposed to help work through the stages. But for me they didn't work at all. They did the opposite.

The more I tried to visualize her, the more they lit my emptiness like a gas leak. It got so I longed for the scorch of that fire. I was addicted to its heat. That's when the drives began.

She appeared to you on those drives?

Not like a ghost. More like the pain was so consuming that all of a sudden I would remember. I could feel it so hard that memories would appear. For a few months I found her everywhere, full of life. But it didn't last. The more time I spent at beaches and playgrounds, parking lots, diners, the less it worked, the more the memories lost their vividness. But it was the pain I was after. That's what was actually going dull, the intensity of it. And without it, I was afraid that I could forget her, that she could be forgotten, in color, even for a second.

Where was the first place you went to see her?

Your old apartment.

Really?

Near the end of the pregnancy, I'd take a bath every night.

I was back with you all by then.

I used to close the door and shut out the world. It would just be her and me, and I'd hold a mirror over my stomach—she'd be weightless inside, which caused her to kick—and I could see the imprint of her foot through my skin. I'd lie there in the water for an hour or so, pushing her foot or hand back inside just to see her push out on the other side, or sometimes even press back against me, like our palms were touching. Sitting there, I'd try to only think positive thoughts and feel happy feelings, trusting that every bit helps, every little effort was worth it, half believing I could protect her by forcing all the negativity out of my mind and body.

You did a good job.

Oh, bullshit.

No, I mean it. You gave her the gift of an imagination.

It was just me being sentimental.

I remember her punching a wall once, and then later on, after she calmed down, I watched her apologize to it.

She did not.

Where you think that came from?

Was that at the old house?

Les nods.

Is that where you would have returned to?

What do you mean?

If you were driving the streets like me.

Yes.

You loved that house.

Why not? It was ours. Bought and paid for by us alone. But I'd go there for a different memory. When Angie was a tot and she'd be up crying at night, I'd lean over the top of her crib to quiet her. There she was, flailing her limbs, and I'd rest my hand on her belly, feeling those baby breaths rise and fall. I'd glide my fingers up her stomach and over her ribs and then back down to her belly, making a tiny figure eight. The truth is that's the only real honest tenderness I can pull up when I think over my life. My fingertips playing over her little body was a boundary I'd never broken with anyone—not a parent, not a friend, not a wife. Just my child.

I'm so mad at you for jumping into that water.

You got a right to be.

It was stupid. In a storm and at night?

I wasn't thinking.

You've always left me behind. You were trying for good this time.

I'm sorry.

Did anything happen to you out there in the water?

Aside from almost freezing to death?

I mean, was it all just fear?

There was a moment when I got past it.

What was that like?

I don't even know.

Please try.

She's thinking about Angie, he realizes, about their daughter's final moments.

Like I was a drop in the ocean, he says, but also like I *was* the ocean.

Marlene retreats into her mind.

You think it's possible that it was neither of our faults? he asks.

No.

Shitty things happen all the time. Random shitty things.

When a child dies, it's always the parents' fault.

Les expels a breath he's been hanging on to this entire conversation.

When we were in Destiny, she says, I figured out why I needed to return. What was calling me back down there. Of course, it had nothing to do with Josie. Or the three of us together. Or any of my stupid plans. That's the final place. The last one. The only spot where I hadn't relived memories of her. You see what I mean? If I remembered Angie there, if memories of her disappeared from Destiny the same way that they had in all the other locations, I'd have no other place to go to see her. I'd have returned to the last place where I could feel all that emptiness and all that pain, the fullness of it, one final time. I'd have made the choice to do that. You see what I'm saying? What I'm trying to say?

Tell me plainer.

It'll mean that I've decided it's OK to heal.

Were you serious the other night about love not being enough?

Don't ask me that question.

Why not?

Let's just assume from now on that if we're here it's because we're willing to try.

Les and Marlene talk like this for hours, until night moves down the walls of the room and light from the hallway seeps through the edges of the door, the TV casting a dull glow. They talk until silence stretches out before them again. But it's not the silence of waiting and wanting. It's a different kind altogether. Les recognizes this silence too. He sees himself back on the stern, surf rod in hand, night tacked up to the sky by an immense spread of stars. The closer you come to another human being, the farther you venture into vast and mystifying waters.

IT'S LATE WHEN Marlene wakes on the chair and climbs into bed with Les. He lifts the sheet and they fold in together. Their breaths find each other. Fast at first, alternating, rhythmic as strolling footsteps. They curl in closer and their breaths align, fall into a slow and slumbering pace.

The next morning they wake facing each other in the hospital bed.

They lie quietly.

Les drinking up her hair, Marlene tracing the lines of his hand.

What are we going to do? he says.

I don't know. What do people do? People who want to start over.

They go west.

That's right, they go west.

Do you want to go west?

No.

The sun paints her cheek with warmth.

There's daylight in your eyes, he says.

SIXTEEN

Through her windshield Marlene observes as The Villas sleeps. She's parked in her usual spot, a block down from the motel. No girls are in the enclosure. No activity at all since she's arrived. From her seat she watched the weep of dew dissolve as the day burned into focus. Les returned home from the hospital a week ago. He's on the mend. But she's not yet received word from Josie, and Marlene has begun to ruminate and worry. Even so, she didn't know she was coming here when she left the apartment an hour ago. She was only stepping out for an errand.

Marlene cuts the engine and steps from her car.

She takes the sidewalk alongside the gate surrounding the empty swimming pool.

She walks up to the entrance, presses her face to the glass.

The lobby is decorated with the crumbling gaudy futurism she should have anticipated: leopard-print seats and sofas, mustard carpeting, chrome swivel stools upholstered in artificial leather, also mustard. Bubble pendant lamps hanging at varying heights like a fleet of flying saucers. The coffee and end tables all kidney beans and cashews. The trample of time recorded in burn marks, stains, and distresses; in failing technologies, too: cigarette machine broken, jukebox broken, a charred plastic palm tree still adorned in a string of half burned-out Christmas bulbs flashing some undecipherable code.

The Villas is emptier than she expects.

Not a person in sight.

She pulls the handle.

The door opens easily.

She enters.

Her heart bright and conductive.

Each step is her last until she takes another.

She reaches the front desk at the end of the short leg of the L-shaped motel. To the right is a little office. She peers inside, shocked by the amount of detritus it contains: There's a little table, a cot, a wall-mounted fan; there are tattered notebooks and torn books; yellowing newspapers; tools as well—wrench, plyers, screwdriver, circular blades but no saw, washers and bolts; milk jugs filled with coins, with screws; broken cheaters missing arms, missing lenses; camping lantern, canned foods; a bottle of hot sauce, cap crusted; a crate of flashlights; several empty pint vodka bottles, the stench of them; brooms; mops; rubber gloves; plunger. The room is lit by a long row of security monitors cycling through images, interior and exterior. A figure rolls over on the cot.

Marlene realizes it's Bill.

She backs away, turns toward the building's long leg. Josie told Marlene about her room. The location is easy enough to recall: back side, second floor, far corner. Marlene opens a glass door, stepping out to the pool. There's relief again outdoors. A number of life-size plastic palm trees rise from lengths of Astroturf that run into miniature golf greens, weaving through cracked wind-mills and lighthouses, dried-up waterfalls and peeling plastic frogs perched on chipped toadstools. She ascends a flight of stairs, makes her way to the top floor on the motel's back end. At every turn she fears the phantoms of her own anticipation.

She walks down the hallway.

The room is unlocked.

Marlene opens the door.

A standard queen like at any other motel: bed bookended by nightstands, a long, low dresser crowned with a TV, minifridge to the side, round table with two chairs by the window AC unit. Marlene walks the space. In the back there's a sink, toilet, and bathtub-shower. She turns just before the mirror, takes in the room from its most cavernous point. Heavy drapes safety-pinned together keep the room in shadow. The red numbers of the digital clock glow dully.

She walks over to a table lamp, flips the switch, sits on the bed.

Marlene recognizes this room all too well, its beyond-time spirit curated haphazardly to the taste of day sleepers, dusk lovers, marauders of night. Here is a place not meant for sustained habitation, one whose best quality is the lingering promise of dawn and departure. A transitional place made hideous by its permanence. Not unlike Marlene's own apartment. Her appeal to these girls, the way they must have seen her, is laid bare: less caretaker, more kin. She now understood why she never wanted to enter The Villas. She'd have seen herself too prominently.

She kept the meter running, Bill says.

Marlene jumps.

He stands in the door.

Marlene's terrified, then apologetic.

But she hears his voice slurred with sadness.

She told the cabdriver to call the cops if she wasn't out in thirty, he goes on.

Marlene takes in his shabby appearance, the bathrobe, sweatpants, and slippers.

His vim dimmed by the vodka he takes from his pocket.

He pulls from the pint bottle.

He walks into the room, sits down next to her, offers her a nip.

Their eyes meet and he double blinks.

Marlene turns away.

I'm not interested in you, he says. We have very different projects in this world.

She takes the bottle and pulls from it.

She said no to me right here. I asked her to marry me.

Marlene looks around the room again, attempting to re-create the moment. Josie sitting Bill down, perhaps oriented just as they are now, explaining her hopes for a new life, tone soft to evoke his reason, not his fury. She catches sight of a soap bar by the sink, a sequined dress in the cracked closet, a pair of clear heals under the nightstand. She reads these details for confirmation of Josie's escape. There's none. But they also do not refute it.

Still, the objects cast her into dark thoughts.

She wouldn't have disappeared without saying goodbye, Marlene tests Bill.

Don't mess with me, Deacon. I know she said goodbye to you.

Bill takes the bottle back.

You did a number on her, he says. I hardly recognized her sincerity. When I first met her, she was bold as a movie star and tough as a street fighter. You could see the fire. Her eyes burning on a walk on the beach, the scrape of her teeth against a fork as she ate, the crack of daylight in my doorway when she snuck into my room to sleep. But it's only the wind, he says.

I don't know what that means.

We saw a deer this once in the woods, me and Josie. Outside of some campsite where we were crashing at the time. The day was so still, nothing moved. We watched this deer bend down to drink at a stream. Then the leaves started to shake and the deer stopped cold, frightened. Imagine that moment. Really imagine for a second. Trying to figure between the wind moving over the water and a mountain lion creeping up behind you. Energy itself, the uncut stuff—you'd be busting open with it. Take a second and place yourself there. Then imagine putting your head back down to the water and continuing to drink.

You're not making any sense.

That's how we live, I remember her saying. Day to day. Believing it's only the wind.

You're telling me she's going to be OK?

I'm trying to say much more than that.

But she's going to be OK?

Of course she will. Goodbye, Deacon.

MARLENE STARTS THE car, rolls the window up. Her eyes sting from cold that swept in while she was inside. The sky is a sheet of hammered metal. She looks at the empty enclosure, stares past it, recalling her first visit to The Villas. Whatever pretense she once had for coming here has vanished. She understands now that her desire to nurture these women was less about relief from their lives or reprieve from her own pain than about her need for cautious connection and control, which she must relinquish. Josie is fine. She's free. She'll drop a note in the mail. She'll call the apartment when she resettles. She will show up out of the blue. Marlene will hear from her soon.

Marlene sees Bill at the front door, exiting the motel.

She pulls forward.

In her rearview she watches him walk into the street after her car, swigging from the pint bottle as he stalks across his decaying kingdom. There is the abandoned fast-food lot where the face of the sign has been torn down, leaving just the electrical bowels of an almond-eye insignia. The empty parkway and pocked roads, the shuttered window fronts and gutted gas stations, the wind rushing around the neon island that soars in the gloom. Traces of life are scant, and yet they threaten to rise up and swallow the place whole. Bare bushes hem in the roads, tree trunks push up sidewalks, vines strangle signposts, the frayed edges of the sea lashing at the shore nearby.

SEVENTEEN

The windows and doors are open at the C-View. The temperature warming in the early afternoon, the scent of brine drifting through the bar from awning to alley. The daylight shows the dim space with unflattering clarity. Fraying lampshades hang askew from the ceiling, black threadbare carpet now discovered to be checkered blue and gray, hangnails of varnish peeling off the bar top, and the luster of the swordfish over the liquor racks faded, the colors cartoonish.

Les's balance remains unsteady, fingers still ghosts.

The injuries did not stop him from helping to plan John Wayne's memorial.

Les, Marlene, and Ethan enter the bar, stay close at the beginning of the event, make their way around the busy room together. China's twins are tearing about and Ethan takes off to join the gang swarming the shuffleboard table. Among the crew exist peculiar measures of distance and restraint. Wives and girlfriends segregate to the buffet table. At the bar, a downcast Alright, reeling from guilt, occupies his usual seat, flanked by Booby, who won't let up on Captain's ear. Hoover and China, pretending to like each other, stand by a blown-up wedding photo of John

Wayne in a tuxedo, discussing the strange hairstyle he sported that day. Monk Man is absent. He still hasn't arrived by the time beers escalate to beers and shots and then to just shots, and Hoover thinks up the idea for the entire bar to drink cosmos in John Wayne's name. Everybody laughing now, loosening up, agreeing, the logic same as ever: anything to touch up the memory with bolder colors, the more outrageous, the better.

When the open bar ends, they collect a pool to buy another hour, and then a third, drinking more and more exotic concoctions: sex on the beaches and beachcombers, painkillers and Palomas, blue Hawaiians and blue lagoons, sakeritas, mai tais, bay breezes, and hurricanes. Alright at one point goes behind the bar to shake up some Burmese mixture he'd read about in one of his war history books. Until the question about John Wayne's hair in the photograph cycles back around to the group as a whole.

Someone please explain why JW looks like he's got a ring around his hair, Hoover shouts. He holds up the blown-up photo.

Looks like a reverse bowl cut, China says.

Or like he got his head stuck on a plunger, calls Booby.

Stray, Alright says, Stray, what's going on with John Wayne's hair?

The bar quiets and looks at him.

He stands on the foot rail to get taller.

The night before his wedding, he says. Then louder, clearing his throat: The night before his wedding we all went out big, right? Well, John Wayne crashed at our place afterward . . . or I crashed at his? he says, looking to Marlene for the answer.

Our place, she says.

Was that the time he pissed himself on the air mattress?

Maybe skip that part, she says.

OK, well, the next morning we woke up late and sick and John Wayne had to get back to his place, showered, dressed, and

to church. We had no time to spare. Still, en route to the cere-
mony, he said he needed to *fortify his gut.* We sat in a booth at
Burger King, John Wayne chewing his Whopper slow like a cow,
and I put together one of those paper crowns and popped it on
his wet head. He didn't take it off until he was about to walk
down the aisle. By then his hair had dried and poofed up like in
the photo. It was like that for the rest of the day, in all the pictures.
I remember thinking in the booth that it suited him, the crown,
like he belonged at a Renaissance festival or something. Like in
another lifetime, he was some big jovial king.

The bar remains silent as Les comes back out of himself.

And then the crew is suddenly being pulled down the sidewalk in the warmest part of the day, the ocean opening before
them, their drunken reveries drawing them to the magnet of the
sea. Ethan and Marlene walk with Alright, Les behind them,
beside China.

Where's Monk today? Les asks.

Skipped town a few weeks ago.

No shit?

You're out of the loop. You hear Lutz is taking away Alright's
boat?

I heard he was retiring.

Too many bad runs. Guess who they're giving the boat to?

You're shitting me? Booby?

And he's keeping Hoover on.

Nobody said anything to Lutz?

China seems surprised by the question.

You should get out, Les says.

Booby offered me a spot, but there's no way. I'm talking to
another captain.

I mean out for good.

You mean like you?

Like go see your family in San Jose.

Work is here, Stray. My family is here.

Or maybe it's not too late to go back to school, you know?

I'll quit fishing at some point.

Not if you keep gambling.

Especially if I keep gambling, China says, laughing.

On the beach the mood changes sharply. There are no ashes to spread, and an edge about how to end the memorial unsettles the bunch.

In the quiet, Les notices Ethan staring off into space.

He realizes the boy is looking at the ocean.

Ethan glances at him, then back to the sea, the soft blue of his eyes turning hard.

Are you afraid of the water? Les asks him.

No, Ethan says.

Les is already hoisting him up, holding him tightly, striding into the ocean. Ethan shrieks when the water touches his ankles and then he laughs as Les continues to wade deeper, the cold rising up his back before they both plunge beneath the waves. He clasps his hands even more firmly around Les's neck as they return to the surface and chart out farther. Les whispers to Ethan that his father is here, will always be here, promises if he just listens he can hear him.

They are silent.

The waves crash on the shore.

That's his breath, Les says.

And Ethan hugs him tighter, saying, Dive, dive, dive, and he does.

Winded again, Les and Ethan come up for air. The sun dances from one wave to the next, blinding them, and they look to the distance, where a bluff of clouds looms over the sea like a faded mountain range. Like the underpainting of another earth. They hear whoops and hollers from behind them, spin around, the crew charging the water, diving into crests, splashing each other, tripping in the sand, laughing riotously. Les watches these fools careen toward the sea.

EIGHTEEN

M arlene stretches out a length of rope, measures it with steps, barefoot in the damp grass. Above her, beneath the flames of sunset, dragonflies pick off the mosquitoes that drove them to the screened porch for supper an hour ago. Soon the bats and barn swallows will descend on the dragonflies. It's a nightly routine Marlene knows well. Meanwhile, she coils the rope over her shoulder, peers inside the house at Les cleaning the dishes in the bright lights of the kitchen. She makes her way to the magnolia, cuts a few switches from a branch with shears, then fashions the switches into a dozen separate stakes, the sweet, dusty scent of the white flowers filling her lungs.

The tide moved out this time on the drive to Destiny. Marlene and Les watched as over the course of several hours and hundreds of miles the water withdrew from the wetlands, a meadow of glinting marsh grass gradually unsheathed. In the shallows, egrets preyed patiently, feet deep in rich peat. And in the depths, where the highway lifted above the flood line, the intracoastal snaked luminous and wide as a river. Marlene saw herself young, the tidal lands in the orbs of her eyes.

Before long the bridge to Destiny rose up over the great canal. Seabirds hung in the high breeze while in the water below children caught the wind in Sunfishes. They turned right onto the county road that curved to Marlene's childhood home. Windows down a bouquet of cut grass drifted into the truck, honeysuckle, lilac, the faint scent of decay off the sea. Overhead, curls of wispy clouds were strewn over the blue.

A letter from Phoenix arrived a few days before they moved their things to storage. Josie had bought a car, driven almost the entire width of the country to visit her mom, which was why it took so long for her to write. She admitted that she didn't know how much more she could handle her mom, or her mom's boyfriend, but she liked the warmth and planned to push on elsewhere soon. In the envelope were newspaper clippings from her drive: intensifying hurricanes in the Gulf, tornado alley widening from the Great Plains to the southeast, droughts from El Niño rising up from the Pacific, blazing wildfires to the West. In each state she passed, Josie collected articles that blamed the smoke from California for hazing over their own perfect little plot of summer sky.

Can I show you something? Marlene says to Les once he's outside.

Sure.

They follow a path that cuts through the center of the field, a makeshift road worn down to dirt tracks by work trucks. The border growth between the different crops still holds some semblance of the field she knows from youth: tall grass to their thighs and purple vetch a shade deeper in the darkening day. Beyond these borders, the long lines of the field alternate between oily greens and the orange and aged dirt. Pollen hovers in the evaporating quiet as the cicadas begin their watery chirp. Marlene stops at the far end of the land, takes out her first stake, and sticks it into the ground. She hands Les one end of the rope, keeping hold of the other, and asks him to walk a straight line east, toward the trees. The rope stretched tight, she tells him to stay put and she walks toward him, driving a stake into the ground by his feet. She continues east until the line is again pulled tight and she puts down a third stake.

Back porch? Les asks.

Marlene nods. She points to the second floor. Main bedroom, she says.

Nice view.

Damn right.

She walks out another length of rope, drives down a fourth stake, calls out, Garage, and turns south to the road. They pace off four more lengths before taking another right, west now, at every stake, announcing the layout: Front door. Hallway. Half bath. Driveway. Garden. Guest room. Living. Dining. Ethan's room.

Don't joke about that, he says.

I'm only kidding.

They're going to find Kathleen.

Who cares? If she's a shitty mom, then who cares?

They put down more stakes, the pace accelerating. They run playfully past one another with the length of rope, as if flinging each other forward. Once they square the plot, all twelve stakes down, they look over their work. Nothing is said about how they'll afford to build or what they're going to do for work. Nothing about calling her parents to apologize, to tell them of their plan to live down here now. Nothing more about Ethan either. He has a room with them if he needs one. Breathlessly they watch their home rise out of the land and stand there.

They return to the house the same way they came.

Les lights the chiminea, sparks two Merits.

Marlene brings out a bottle of smoky rum.

They sit together beneath the sheltering sky.

Listen, can you hear that? Marlene says.

Les struggles to separate the sounds, unlike Marlene, who knows these summer nights so well. The crickets and katydids have joined with the cicadas, the combination receding to the background despite the volume. Other hidden noises resonate: the crack of wood, the clink of ice, the hiss of the chiminea, the leaves and grass gone quiet, a breeze abruptly still.

You can't hear it? I think there's four or five of them. No, wait, more. Listen for it.

Les shakes his head.

Vroo-vroo-vroo, she chants. Vroo-vroo-vroo.

She watches Les become aware of the low-pitch drone of the bullfrogs as it emerges from out of the insect sound. The noise rises, louder and louder, *Vroo-vroo-vroo, vroo-vroo-vroo*, growing in vibration, too, like the bellow of a string orchestra.

How many are out there? he asks.

Two dozen, maybe three. I don't know.

What do you want to do about them?

Let them be.

They're a plague.

No they're not.

Sure they are.

Then who's Pharaoh?

What's that?

If they're a plague, then who's Pharaoh?

Marlene's voice drowns into the rhythmic unison and she marks her own ease about the pulse trembling all around them. She squeezes Les's hand and lets it fall. In that sound, in that song, she allows the vibration to roll over her, impress a weight onto her skin, as if it has taken shape, become somehow solid.

As if she were suddenly subsumed in the music of raw matter. When she closes her eyes, the red-winged blackbirds plummet unexpectedly from the sky, the horseshoe crabs turn from their eggs that scatter in the wind, the bullfrogs groan over a long journey with grit left to endure longer. Angie is here, too, her swirl of ashes taken in by the sweep and surge of the sea. We remain in a state of perpetual displacement while always, in the end, returning home.

ACKNOWLEDGMENTS

First, to my editor, Daniel Loedel, whose luminous notes north-starred the revision of this novel—I am indebted for your direction, friendship, and support; to my agent Bill Clegg, whose wisdom over multiple drafts always urged me back to the desk with the confidence required to fail better; to Babak, Cady, Hannah, Josh, Jude, Olivia, Stephen, Tom, and especially Ragav, for the generosity of your time and the significance of your remarks; to Brady, Chris, Curt, Eric, Jeff, Keith, Neill, Randy, and the crew of the *Jersey Cape*—without you all, this book would have little credibility; to my students, for continuing to hone the precision of my thinking; to Centro Studi Americani in enchanted Roma, for giving me a workplace when I needed one the most; and to Justine, my first and last reader, my friend and guide, *when I touch you . . . it's with hands that are dying and resurrected.*

A NOTE ON THE AUTHOR

Daniel Magariel is an author from Kansas City. *One of the Boys*, his first novel, a *New York Times Book Review* Editors' Choice and Amazon Best Book of 2017, was translated into eight languages and shortlisted for the Lucien Barrière prize. He has a BA from Columbia University as well as an MFA from Syracuse University. He teaches at Columbia University. Magariel lives in Cape May, New Jersey.